ALONE AT NINETY FOOT

ALONE

AT

NINETY

FOOT

KATHERINE HOLUBITSKY

ORCA BOOK PUBLISHERS

Copyright © 1999 Katherine Holubitsky

No part of this book may be reproduced, stored in a retrieval system,
or transmitted, in any form or by any means, without the prior
written permission of the publisher, except by a reviewer who
may quote brief passages in review.

Canadian Cataloguing in Publication Data
Holubitsky, Katherine, 1955 –
Alone at Ninety Foot

ISBN 1-55143-127-0 (bound) — ISBN 1-55143-129-7 (pbk.)

1. Death — Juvenile fiction.   I. Title.
PS8565.O645A73 1999   jC813'.54   C99-910036-X
PZ.H743A1 1999

Library of Congress Catalog Card Number: 98-83008

Orca Book Publishers gratefully acknowledges the support of our
publishing programs provided by the following agencies: the Department
of Canadian Heritage, The Canada Council for the Arts, and the British
Columbia Arts Council.
Canadä

Cover design by Christine Toller
Cover illustration by Ljuba Levstek
Printed and bound in Canada

IN CANADA:
Orca Book Publishers
PO Box 5626, Station B
Victoria, BC Canada
V8R 6S4

IN THE UNITED STATES:
Orca Book Publishers
PO Box 468
Custer, WA   USA
98240-0468

01 00 99   5   4   3   2   1

For Jeff,
with love
and especially for Max and Paul

ONE

May 25th

My name is Pamela Mary Collins. I am fourteen years old and I am lying on the white rock, suntanning, down by Ninety Foot. I should be in English class but Mr. Bartell was picking on me again and I didn't want to see his face. Besides, I just need to be alone.

I am lying very still with my eyes closed against the sun. I feel like I am melting in my gym shorts, turning liquid, blending, baking into the surface of the granite, becoming part of it. And in time, if I lie here long enough, the mountain junipers will crack me open and work their way through me. They will bring the soil from out of me and root themselves, right here, next to Ninety Foot.

Ninety Foot is this natural pool in Lynn Creek, which runs through Lynn Canyon. It is called that because of the sheer rock walls that rise ninety feet high on either side of it. Down here where I am, at the bottom of the gorge, the water is clear and green and it is cold. So cold, it is painful. It also moves amazingly fast because just before Ninety Foot the canyon narrows. Massive volumes of surging water have to squeeze through a slim gap in the rocks.

Lynn Creek begins as snowmelt high up in the mountains north of Vancouver. It mixes with rainfall and tumbles down the mountain. It crashes through the rainforest. It thunders into this canyon. It pounds against the polished granite, exploding from pool to pool. And if you're not used to it, I mean the rushing and the thundering and the violence of it all, it can be frightening.

But I am used to it. I have been coming to Lynn Canyon Park all my life. I can't see it from where I am, but the suspension bridge crosses the gorge about a quarter-mile down the canyon. And a long way past that is a smaller wooden bridge that crosses the creek just above the water. It's a bit out of the way, but when I want to get to the other side of the gorge, that's the route I take.

I used to cross the suspension bridge. When I was

young and we were on it alone, my mom and I would stop in the middle. Lynn Creek was a thousand miles below us, cutting its way through the rock as it has for a zillion or whatever years. I used to feel sort of invincible swaying in the air above it. Like I was capable of anything. Like I could even fly up there with the peregrine falcons. Sometimes I scared myself by thinking that I might try. Right away, my knees would go weak and I'd grip tighter to the cable railing. Once, I told my mom what I was feeling. She said I shouldn't worry. It was just my flight of fancy testing my common sense. My common sense would always win out.

It is a dangerous place though. And many people have died here. People have jumped from the bridge. One girl was killed while suntanning. Much like I'm doing right now. Out of the blue, a giant boulder bounced down the cliff and crushed her. Drunken teenagers have hopped the chain-link fence and fallen into the gorge. People have drowned, held beneath the surface by powerful currents. Right here in Ninety Foot pool. Murdered bodies have been found rotting alongside the fallen cedars, tangled in ferns and vines. Then there were some who just walked up the mountain and were never seen again.

But I like it here. When I was in grade seven, we studied the art of Emily Carr. We went to see her paintings at the Vancouver Art Gallery. Back then I didn't think they looked very real. They were all so, like, dark

3

and haunting. The earth heaved up and the skies hung down. And the trees swelled like purple waves. They were not straight lines and triangles like I thought trees in the forest should be.

I have sat here for many hours since then and I think I understand why she did them like that. She was giving them life by painting them as if they were moving. The forest, the sky, the water – even the rocks seemed to move.

But what I remember more than her paintings was something our teacher read from her journals. About how when you sit in a forest everything appears still. But it isn't really. If you listen and watch closely, life is happening everywhere around you. It's only that the growth happens so slowly that you can't see it. Like seeds popping open and leaves unfurling and insects burrowing under the soil. In silence, life keeps raging on.

I guess that's why I like to come here. I never feel lonely. I've tried to get the same feeling sitting quietly in my room. But nothing ever grows in there. Except, as my dad would say, the pile of laundry in the corner and the dust bunnies under my bed.

"They could hold their own against a pack of greyhounds," he says.

My friends – and believe me, I don't have many – think I'm a hermit coming to sit down here by myself. I've tried to explain how nice it can be just to sit in the quiet of the forest. They look at me like I've grown a beard or something, so I don't mention it anymore.

Like I said, I don't have many friends. But then, that's nothing new. I never have. When I was little, my mom was my best friend. I'm an only child. I did have a sister once — for eight months when I was nine. Her name was April. I don't remember very much about her except that she was always wet. They used to tell me how much she looked like me when I was a baby. I didn't see the resemblance. I have one picture with us together. I am squinting into the sun, holding her on the swing in our backyard. She is hidden behind giant sunglasses. I remember when that picture was taken. I was ticked off because she was wet, and even though Mom knew it, she was forcing me to sit there while she took the picture. She thought it was the most adorable thing she'd ever seen. Yeah, right. A pee-soaked lap is truly adorable. Then two days later April died of sudden infant death syndrome. It's called SIDS for short and it's when a baby just stops breathing.

When I was very little, before April, Mom used to take me for walks on the far side of the canyon. We'd cross the suspension bridge and follow the old logging trails partway up the mountain, picking salmon- and huckleberries along the way. We both wore silver bells to scare away the black bears. We never actually saw any, but we stepped over plenty of droppings full of seeds. So we knew they were there. Of course, I imagined I saw them. Or at least their shadows darting with the light among the Douglas fir. But then, I imagined I saw a lot of things. I imagined I saw ghostly creatures rising from the fallen cedars. And I imagined evil beasts crouching in the hollows, waiting to pounce on little girls.

Mom would break off root licorice from the moss that grows on the vine maples and peel it for me to try. I didn't think it tasted much like licorice. But then, I also didn't think the yellow skunk cabbage smelt like a skunk. In fact, I thought it was quite a beautiful plant and didn't think it deserved such an offensive name. Almost every time, Mom would make a new discovery. Once she found a tiny sprig of wild holly and you'd think she'd won a billion dollars.

Mom taught me how to make wreathes and ornamental trees with the pine cones we collected. She also taught me how to bead. When I was six, I heard the bell for school when I was still half a block away. I don't know why, I guess because I've always been shy and I didn't want everyone looking at me when I walked in late, but I turned around and ran home. Mom didn't even get mad. When the school called, she told them I had stomach cramps. I would be there after lunch. Then she taught me how to bead a simple bracelet. We didn't talk about it, but it was like we were partners or something that morning.

I got pretty good at beading. I do fairly intricate patterns now. I've made a lot of jewelry and belts and some purses. Not too long ago, I beaded the neckline of a plain white blouse.

I have another hobby too. Whenever I go anywhere, I like to bring back a living piece of the place I've been. So I collect water or, where there is none, unusual stones, flowers or even soil. I keep them in April's baby-food jars. It's quite amazing how many mushy peas and carrots a kid can eat in just eight months. But the jars are just the right size.

I have water from The Lost Sea, this cool lake deep in the caves outside Knoxville, Tennessee, where my uncle lives. I have a jar of the Atlantic Ocean, which tastes the same as the Pacific. I have white sand from Sanibel Island, which is off the coast of Florida. We went there three years ago for Christmas holidays. I have red earth from Red Rock Park near Medicine Hat. And I have lots of local ones too, like a crumbled sand dollar from Cates Park and an arbutus leaf from Lighthouse Park. But those aren't nearly so exotic. Those were the first I collected.

I like these scraps of nature. More than pictures. Pictures are flat and dead and become dated so you get bored looking at them. It is the smells and the tastes and the feel of a place that makes it a part of you.

I stayed with my aunt and uncle for two weeks after April died. Mom was in the hospital and Dad was forever working. He's an accountant. When he was at home, he was visiting Mom.

After she came home, it was a long time before we walked in Lynn Canyon again. When we did, Mom wasn't nearly as much fun as she was before April. She didn't look around, but walked straight ahead, with her eyes on the path. Dad said she had trouble concentrating and was depressed about April. But so was I.

Emily Carr says, "Nothing is dead. Not even a corpse. It moves into the elements when the spirit has left."

I told this to Mom, thinking it might make her feel better about April. But she just kept on peeling carrots. I'm not even sure she heard me.

I wonder what they're doing in English. Probably Mr. Bartell is reading a passage from *Lord of the Flies*, which we're studying. He has this pompous, affected way of reading to us. And then he stands smugly, waiting for a reaction. Like we should give him credit or something for these great works of literature. Like if it weren't for him, we wouldn't have the intelligence to discover them ourselves. Or like he even wrote them. As if.

His scraggy beard and bug eyes give me the creeps. Sometimes, when he gets real excited and his face turns red reading Shakespeare or something, I'm afraid that if he got knocked on the back, those eyeballs might pop right out and come rolling down the aisle.

And he's always trying to suck up to the popular kids. Like Danielle Higgins. She's blond and perky and petite. Not like me, a hundred feet tall with arms and legs dangling like a vine maple. He laughs at her jokes and marks questions she answered the same as me right, when I was marked wrong. Teachers like that are so lame. What they don't realize is that the popular kids still think they're losers.

Last fall my best friend since kindergarten, Joanne Robertson, got asked to one of Danielle's parties. And somehow, I got dragged along. Her parents were out of town and her eighteen-year-old brother was supposed to be looking after her. He was in the canyon at a bush party. Danielle was offering everyone her parents' booze, mixing it with Orange Crush and gulping it down by the tumblerful. I had one taste and nearly puked on the spot. Joanne drank two beer and a glass of Kahlua. She started acting like a complete moron, belching like a seal and smoking two cigarettes at once.

Then Danielle turned off the lights. People started pairing off, necking all over the floor and in the bedrooms. Even Joanne ended up with Carl Jenkins. I guess she was so drunk she'd forgotten his claim to fame was blowing a fart so loud Mr. Bartell called the custodian to check out the heating ducts.

So I was left alone, swallowed into a bean bag in the family room, listening to the sweating and grunting and sucking noises in the dark around me. People can be such pigs. But I couldn't move without drawing attention to the fact that I was unclaimed. Although, believe me, if you saw what was left, you would know it was by choice. Finally, I got up the nerve, and after tripping over several bodies which didn't notice me anyway, I made it to the front door. I put on my shoes and went home.

Joanne really burned me. She'd told her mother she was staying at my house. She never did come home with me. She spent the night at Danielle's, being cool. And she got away with it.

I'll never be cool. I don't even want to be. Not if I have to get drunk as a monkey and make an idiot out of myself to do it. I have some pride.

I wonder sometimes what it is that makes us want everybody to like us. When I think about it, there are so few people that I really like being with, why should I expect that everyone should like being with me? I don't even like to talk all that much. I mostly keep my thoughts to myself. I guess, when it comes right down to it, I don't even like being around people.

Emily Carr was a lot like that. She preferred her dogs and monkey and her white rat to the company of most people. I think Emily and I would have made very good friends. We could have sat in the camaraderie of the forest for hours, not speaking, she working at her painting and me beading, only stopping to comment now and again on the color of a lady-slipper or a shift in the wind or a change in the sky. Communicating in silence through our crafts. We might even consult one another.

"I just can't capture the mood of that little spruce over there," she might say. "Take a look, Pam. What do you think?"

And I'd set my beading aside and study her painting. "I'm impressed with the unity of movement," I'd say, not because I know the least thing about art, but because I read that is what she aimed for. "I think it looks just fine, Emily."

Joanne was cool for about a month. Then one Saturday she forced me to go to the mall with her and Danielle. God, it was boring hanging around the food court while Danielle flirted with all the guys. And Joanne tried to. Anyway, we were walking past Fairweather's and I saw this really gorgeous peach sweater in the window.

"Try it on," said Joanne.

"No," I said. "I don't have any money."

"So? At least you'll know how it looks on you."

Danielle was still in the food court, so the two of us went inside. This thirty-whatever woman with these giant fat lips opened the fitting-room door for us. Joanne came in with me. "No kidding, Pam. It looks incredible on you. I think you should get it."

"I told you, I don't have any money. And my dad

says I can't get any new clothes until the end of next month." I pulled the sweater over my head and tossed it to Joanne to fold while I put my shirt back on. And then, I couldn't believe it, but she started ripping off the tags.

"What are you doing?"

"They can't pin it on you if there are no tags to prove it was theirs."

"Pin what on me? Joanne? What are you doing?"

She didn't say anything. She just mashed the sweater in a ball, opened my purse and stuffed it in. The tags lay scattered all over the floor.

"Come on," she said, grabbing my arm. "Let's go." At the same time as she threw my purse at me, she yanked me out the door. I had no choice but to walk stiffly, and swiftly, I might add, out into the mall.

"Joanne, this is so wrong."

I could have smacked her over the head, scratched her eyes out, I was so mad at her. I was hurtling through the crowd like a bowling ball not sure of its lane. Then a hand clamped on my shoulder, nearly sending me into a somersault. I was spun around by it, to face the fat-lipped sales clerk.

"Let's have it," she demanded.

Another clerk came up next to her. They glared at me accusingly. They stood as if they were ready to pounce on me if I bolted — or, if necessary, defend themselves if I attacked. I felt as loathsome as a twelve-inch slug.

I couldn't possibly deny I had taken it. Not when I was holding the flaming evidence in my hot little hand. I opened my purse and gave them the sweater. Through the tears racing from my eyes, I could see Joanne, standing in the doorway of a shoe store, watching the confession of a thief with the rest of the crowd. At that moment, I hated her more than I had ever hated anyone.

"Is this what it takes to be popular!" I wanted to shriek. "Is this what it takes to be noticed? That you reduce yourself to a slimy cheat? You fool, Joanne. You stupid fool. I'd rather be one pale grain in a twenty-mile stretch of sand than the one that catches the sun, if this is how you do it."

The clerk took the sweater. She asked me my name. In front of all those people, I stammered it out. I told her my entire three-piece name. It didn't even occur to me to make one up! I then slobbered on about how I'd never done anything like this before and would never do it again. Like, no duh. It was pretty obvious what an incompetent thief I was. She told me to make sure I didn't and then left me, quivering like a jellyfish, to slither home and consider what a poor excuse for a human being I was.

For a month I raced Dad for the telephone. I was terrified that the store clerk would change her mind and look me up, determined that my father should know what a delinquent child he had raised.

Dad laughed, thinking I had a boyfriend. To tease me, he would sometimes beat me in the race. He didn't know how freaked I was when he said hello.

Joanne never apologized, but instead she became annoyingly nice, oozing over things like my hair, which was the same, long and brown, as it had always been. Or a couple of times she bought me stuff in the cafeteria that I didn't even want. Like this gross raisin pudding that I wouldn't feed to a dog. Finally, I told her to quit groveling, that I forgave her, but what she had done was a really jerky thing to do.

She agreed that it was.

A few weeks later I noticed that she and Danielle didn't hang out much anymore.

"We didn't really have a lot in common," Joanne told me. "Besides, she has so many friends, she doesn't need me."

I've watched Danielle since then. Know what I discovered? It isn't that she has a lot of friends — she just goes through a lot of friends. She uses people like Kleenex, then tosses them aside when she is finished with them.

I have the goose bumps. I look up to see a thick swatch of gray cloud hovering above the canyon — and me. There's not much point in lying here now. Besides, it's almost noon. I suppose I should go home, make some lousy sandwich or something and head back to school. We start social dance in gym after lunch. Both the boys' and girls' classes have to take it together. The thing is, they make it so we get thirty percent of this term's mark just for showing up. Like anyone would go if they didn't use bribery. I know I wouldn't. If it weren't for my dad. I figure he's been through enough the last few years without me screwing up big time on my report card.

The whole thing about school is that, like I said before, I like to be alone. But I hate being lonely. And I mostly seem to be lonely around people. I'm always lonely at school. I'm lonely on a bus, or in the doctor's office, or even eating dinner at Nana Jean's with the whole family around me. Sometimes, I sit in class, with that talking head at the front, and I imagine my desk sinking slowly through the floor. And after I'm gone the other desks shift, like in some kind of dream sequence, to cover my spot. And no one is the wiser. No one even notices I'm gone. Particularly the head still talking at the front.

I grab my backpack, jump the rocks and start up the path leading to the canyon parking lot. It's straight uphill all the way. The earth forms tall steps where it is trapped by roots and compacted by feet and time. It's quite a stretch, but soon I'm looking down on a part of the gorge where water pours into a smooth tank, much like a granite toilet bowl. It looks very tropical. The water so green and ivy dripping from the rock shelves above — you'd almost expect to see parrots fly by. But you have to be real confident to jump into that pool. And I'm not. It's way too dangerous. Which is why this whole area is restricted. Besides, it's directly below the suspension bridge. I never look up. It gives me the creeps.

I have been studying this area very closely for the last year, noticing this bunch of ferns and that burst of buds. I wish I'd paid more attention in the past. You know, stopped and smelled the roses. Maybe taken a few pictures. That way I'd know what was new growth and what had been here before. I wouldn't have to wonder about that huckleberry bush next to the chain-link fence. Like, was it there a year ago last Tuesday when Mom jumped off the bridge, or has it grown there since? Just a warning for future reference. Never be like me and take things for granted. All this forest around me and I've never really paid attention to it. I doubt there are forests like this anywhere you go in the world. I know for a fact there are no forests like this on Sanibel Island. Or in Medicine Hat. Could I describe it to someone in those places? Yeah, it's green, the trees are tall and there are slugs ten feet long on the paths. Big deal. That doesn't say anything about the way the tree trunks are so thick, your whole class could stand in a ring around them and still not be able to hold hands. Or about the way the rain rolls from the big floppy leaves onto your head after a storm until you're soaked through to the skin. Or how the smell of cedar warms you as the sun stretches its long rays through the Douglas fir to dry out the ground. My point is, it's important to remember details. Of course, if I were Emily Carr, I could just paint it. No words would be needed then.

I know what you're thinking. Why are you going on like that when your mother jumped off the suspension bridge? Sometimes I wonder that myself. But I don't really have a choice, do I? And of course, more importantly to you, you're wondering why she did it. Can't answer that one either. My dad tried to explain that it had something to do with the way she felt after we lost April. I've always wanted to ask him more, but every time I try to, I can see he might just about fall apart. I know he tries real hard to be strong for me. So I don't want to be the one to push and make him crack. He's got to feel he's a support to someone in his life. The school counselor, Mrs. Dalrymple, told me basically the same thing about Mom. She was very, very depressed. But I, for one, can only think that for some reason her common sense didn't kick in that day. She must have felt good, invincible up on that bridge, hundreds of feet above the pool. Like she could fly with the peregrine falcons. And I guess that old flight of fancy just won out.

TWO

May 26th

This is just so unreal I can't believe it. Guess who's teaching us social dance? Mr. Bartell! Ms. Turner, our regular gym teacher, says he puts her to shame. That next to him, she looks like Mr. Bean on the dance floor. So, lucky us, he's offered to take the dance unit. Well, I know I, for one, am ecstatic.

The man is multitalented. He can quote Robert Frost one minute and do the tango the next. I don't believe this. This is obscene. She's actually introducing him and he's waltzing across the floor, kicking his legs. Who does he think he is? If he starts to moonwalk, I'm out of here. He's smiling like a hyena. Don't have a major heart attack, Mr. Bartell. I can guarantee we're not going to be tripping over each other to give you mouth-to-mouth. How can anyone be so happy about making such a fool out of himself?

He tells us we're going to learn the fox trot first. John Robbel wants to know what's the point of learning something straight out of the dark ages. Danny Kim wants to know if he's trying to turn us into pansies. Shauna Whittaker tells him there's no way she'll dance with just any geek in the class and if he doesn't let her choose her own partner, she'll go to Mrs. Lofts. Darla Miller says that it would probably be some kind of abuse or harassment or something if he forced us to.

Mr. Bartell is quiet while we all protest. But I can see something brewing behind his great bug eyes. Then to all of us he booms in his loudest Shakespeare-reading voice, "You'll do it because I said so!"

That basically shuts us up until after he's taken attendance, when he gets that hyena grin again and teaches us stuff like movement and rhythm and partner positions and step combinations and whatever. Then he tells us we have to break into partners, at which point we all groan.

"Pair up with the boy or girl, as the case may be, who has the same last initial as your own. Or," he adds, "the closest to it."

"This is sooo juvenile," Joanne whines.

Mr. Bartell claps his hands, because none of us have moved one inch. "Come on, come on, people. I'm guessing you all passed kindergarten or you wouldn't be here. It's not too hard to figure out. Let's see, B, B, B — no B's. C, C — Miss Collins — "

I am going to die. I am actually going to die right here on the spot. No kidding. Mr. Bartell is walking toward me. Mr. Bartell is bowing to me. Mr. Bartell is taking hold of my hand!

"May I request this dance?"

This is truly *the* single most humiliating event of my entire life. I wish I'd stayed down at Ninety Foot. I wish I'd tripped on a root and broken my foot. I wish I'd been kidnapped by a UFO and forced to submit to inhumane experiments. Anything other than having to dance with Mr. Bartell. I can't even look at him, let alone remember what he just taught us.

"Miss Collins?"

I can hear Joanne and my other so-called friends snickering.

"Huh?"

"May I request this dance?"

Like, do I have a choice?

"I guess so," I mumble into my hair.

Mr. Bartell turns toward the class and bellows half an inch from my ear, "Now, gentlemen! What have I just demonstrated?"

No one has a clue what the answer is.

"It's called proper etiquette, gentlemen! It is proper etiquette to ask for the privilege to dance with your partner. Now I want you all to demonstrate proper etiquette and the young ladies will respond accordingly."

There's all this shuffling around, which I don't really see because I'm too busy staring at the floor, but, like, all thirty guys repeat what Mr. Bartell asked me. With the enthusiasm of a bunch of dead cod, I might add. I'm not sure what the proper responses are supposed to be, but mostly I hear answers like, "Get serious," and "Alright, but only because I need the marks."

Mr. Bartell drags me to the CD player, starts this majorly bad music, if you can even call it that, and while he jerks me back and forth and around and around, hollers out orders to the class. "Alright people, the box step! Eight counts. Quick, quick, quick, quick!"

His breath is like the worst swamp in the deepest depths of Borneo and he's sweating on my head.

"Forward! Touch! Side! Together!"

I wish I were made of mercury. I could slip right out of his arms, slither across the gym and roll out the door.

"Backward! Touch! Side! Together!" Grunt, grunt. "Miss Collins." There is a moldy blast in my face and I realize he is talking to me.

"Yes?" I say.

"You should look at your partner."

Mr. Bartell, the point here is, I don't want to. Now

I suppose if you looked like Matt Damon, it's possible I could work up the nerve. But you are fifteen galaxies away from looking like him, so I'd really rather not.

I have to try real hard to look at him.

"Once more through, class. Count one! You weren't in English class this morning?"

I have to look at him this time, because I'm not sure if he's talking to me or if the question is part of this bizarre dance ritual. Realizing it isn't, and with my imagination stifled because of the, u-hum, air in here, I say, "I went home with a headache."

"I see. Count two. Left and right feet together. And are you feeling better?"

Hold on. I mean, wait just a minute here. Is this proper etiquette? Are you allowed to discuss someone's skipping out when you're dancing with them? Or their personal health?

"Yes," I say, "I feel better."

"Excellent. Step to your right! Your weight onto your right! We will be discussing the final chapters on Wednesday. Be sure to read them. Good job! Everyone bow to their partner and be sure to practice your box step for next class."

What are the chances?

THREE

I am standing with Joanne and Mandeep Gill on the steps after school. There are disgusting blobs of gob all over the cement. By the way, before I say anything further, that's something I want to set straight right now. This may come as a surprise to any of you guys who might read this, but hucking gob is definitely not cool. It is definitely not the least bit attractive, and I don't know whatever gave you the notion that it is. Really, like I want to be sliding on your body fluids everywhere I walk? Keep it in mind.

Danielle Higgins is standing on the sidewalk below us, circled, as always, by a ring of guys. One of them says something and she throws her head back and laughs loudly. He also laughs, plunks his hands on his hips, turns his head and hucks one across the sidewalk. Give me a break. Was it really that hysterical, Danielle? She thinks of more ways to get noticed than Dennis Rodman.

Excuse me. Hang on. There's something different about this picture. The guy with his arm around her waist? I've never seen him before. Not that I pay much attention to guys anymore, but if I did, that one is definitely worth paying attention to. He's got a wicked grin. And a build to die for, and tall — a definite plus for me. He's got short hair, a muscular neck, wide back and I like the way he stands with just a bit of a stoop to his shoulders. Slightly apologetic for his, shall I say, remarkable physique? When he laughs —

"YUM- MY," Joanne rudely interrupts my thoughts. "Where was he when we had to social dance yesterday? My, my. Danielle's really outdone herself this time." Joanne pulls a pack of cigarettes from her backpack and while she continues to drool over Danielle's latest, removes one from the package, snaps a lighter and takes a deep drag. "Still," she says, turning away, exhaling, dropping the cigarette to her side, "I suppose if you're going to deliver the goods, it gives you that much more of a choice."

"When are you going to quit that?" I say.

Joanne knows exactly what I'm talking about, but instead of answering me, she deliberately takes another drag. "As we've discussed before, this is the only bad habit left over from that period, which you have chosen to name my 'dark days.' It could have been much worse."

"It's not healthy."

She taps the ashes onto the cement. "True. But there are many things more unhealthy. Say, playing in traffic, diving in a pool with no water, or standing in a field in the middle of a thunderstorm."

Mandeep laughs.

Joanne continues to smoke. "There's walking on thin ice and challenging a bull to a race. Eating pink hamburger and petting a rabid dog — "

"Getting your teeth X-rayed without the lead apron," pipes in Mandeep.

We both look at her. She shrugs.

"Yeah, there's that," continues Joanne, "and don't forget not buckling your seat belt, not wearing a life jacket, outrunning trains and jumping from a ten-storey building ..."

Joanne goes silent. She stares at Mandeep. Mandeep stares back. Slowly, she begins to shake her head. Joanne turns to me, drops her cigarette to the step and squashes it with her toe. "I'm real sorry, Pam. It just came out. You know I didn't mean anything by it."

"Yeah, yeah, I know." Which was true. But I hated dealing with this be-really-careful-of-what-you-say-around-Pam-or-she'll-spaz attitude. That was one of the things about my mother jumping from the bridge that burned me. It instantly made me into some kind of freak. Some kind of fragile being that had to be tip-toed around so I wouldn't shatter at the slightest word. It made me a special case. And as I think I've mentioned before, I have never liked to stand out.

The day I returned to school after the funeral, it was, like, everyone was *so* nice. The teachers all gave me hugs. Joanne carried my backpack and stuck by me like a crutch. She interrogated anyone who came close to talk to me, demanding their motives before they could speak. Even Sarah McMurtry, who hadn't talked to me since I cut her Barbie doll's hair when we were four, scrambled to pick up my pen when I dropped it during French. I hated it. I hated being singled out and I hated the shifting eyes and the hush that fell over my friends when I approached.

"It's just that, well, no one knows what to say," Joanne told me. "I mean, like, well — you know — okay, it happened like this."

And she told me what happened the day they found out my mom had jumped off the suspension bridge.

I'm going to have to interrupt for one minute here before I tell Joanne's story. I'm going to tell you about crossing the suspension bridge. Then, what she had to say will make more sense. Okay, it's like this:

Crossing the Lynn Canyon suspension bridge is not just strutting onto this wooden structure that's at the same level as the ground you've been walking on. It's more like, sort of, this event. When you first stand high up on the platform leading onto the bridge you get this rush. You suck your breath in because you are not only standing where the bridge begins, but at the very spot where the gorge drops a hundred and sixty feet to the creek. And although you know in your head that swinging bunch of cable, wood and chicken wire has not fallen down yet, common sense tells you it's not smart to walk off the edge of a cliff. So you stand there, looking across to the other side, then down at how you're supposed to get there. Now, because the bridge has this major dip in it, you clamp your hands to the cables on each side and you don't step so much, but more like dive onto it. At first, you try to control your speed, but the bridge drops steeply into the gorge and your feet get away from you. That's why they've added these strips of wood that act like speed bumps. It can be swinging pretty wildly, so you may or may not want to stop in the middle, depending on your strength of nerve. Then you begin to climb up the other side. You go slower because of how steeply it rises, but you're also feeling good that you're more than halfway there. You have to work hard, hanging tightly to the cables to pull you up, using the speed bumps to brace your feet. And there you are. Safe, with the bridge swinging in the canyon behind you.

Now, that's if you do it alone. That's become a rarity. Tourists love the suspension bridge. They love to cross it in herds. You can just imagine how it pitches back and forth with lots of people on it. Especially if you get some wise guy that figures he needs to stand in the middle and heave on the cables to turn it into some kind of ride.

But now, Joanne's story:

It was like this. Mrs. Dalrymple came in to tell us about your mom during social class and, like, no one could believe it! All day, that's all anybody could talk about. Everyone cried and said how awful it was and how we felt so sorry for you and for your dad. And then after school, we were sitting under the cover next to the bike stands when Carol Sanchez said that the worst person to lose in the world would be her mother. That started it.

Some of the guys disagreed with her and that got everyone talking. Linda Yip insisted it would be much worse for her if it was her grandmother. John Robbel said it would have to be his father. Danielle said it would definitely be her sister. Everyone talked louder. Then Tony Lasserman seemed to get mad and said he couldn't care less about his mother, but he never wanted to lose his brother. Danny Kim said he'd pay to have someone take out his brother. By then, the talking had turned to shouting. Suddenly, Mike Ortega stood up and shouted above everyone else, "Yeah, but jumping off the suspension bridge would be the worst way to go!"

This made everybody go quiet. Of course, we had all been thinking about that, but nobody had said it. I mean, you know how scary it is up there and how when we were kids we used to talk about what it would be like to fall off? All the things we'd imagine? What it would be like to let go and fall into nothing. Would you pass out? Would you be killed by hitting the canyon walls on the way down? Would you get impaled on a tree? Would you bounce at the bottom or just go splat? I guess silently we were all thinking these things.

Tony Lasserman was the first to break the silence. "Do you think they got all of her?"

We all looked at him. It was like he knew what we were thinking.

"Well, you know as well as I do, they couldn't just pick her up and carry her out. They'd have to scrape her off. Maybe they didn't get all of her?"

"We thought seriously about this," Joanne told me. "Mike Ortega got all excited. "What if she broke into a whole bunch of pieces? What if they missed one? A foot? Or an eyeball or something?"

John Robbel began to unlock his bike. "There might still be brains stuck to the rock."

At this point Linda Yip told them how disgusting they were being. How they didn't have one manner between them and that it was not only morbid, but in extremely bad taste to discuss the physical condition of the dead.

They considered this for maybe half of a second. Mike ran to the bike stand and jumped on his bike. "Maybe her hair caught in one of the cables and her head is still swinging beneath the bridge!" He tore off and so did all of us behind him."

Joanne continued.

"It was raining that day and half of us fell on the way there, slipping in mud puddles and tripping over our own feet. We were like this frenzied pack, pounding along the road, past the ecology center, past the concession stand and down the steps to the foot of the bridge. Nobody stopped, they just kept on going, screaming and hollering as they stampeded over the edge and poured onto the bridge. Except me. I was the last. I stood at the foot, barely able to breathe, my heart whacking at my chest. I couldn't do it. If there was something to see, I didn't want to see it. I loved your mom, Pam. She was the best. Instead, I followed the fence a hundred feet down the gorge, where I could see them lined up along the bridge. They stretched from one end to the other. And you know what I heard? I heard that piercing shriek of the gulls above me. I heard the splash of rain on the leaves around me. I heard the rush of water falling far, far below me. But not a sound came from that still bridge. Not the creak of a cable. Not a single word spoken. Only terrified silence. What I saw was a row of small frightened faces strung across the canyon. Looking into the gorge that swallowed your mother. And I guess that's why nobody knew what to say to you, Pam.

FOUR

My dad has a new girlfriend. Her name is Jennifer
Reid and she's some kind of big banker. She wears
these technical suits and this real severe hair. Aside
from those things, there's got to be something majorly
wrong with her. The thing is, she's forty years old and
has never been married. That's an entire lifetime without any takers. Whatever her problem is, it's not glaring.
But I'm going to find out.

This is Dad's third attempt. The first one was sort
of nondescript, just this lady he met through work. I
didn't see much of her. I think he was embarrassed to
bring her home. As far as I could figure, it only lasted
a few weeks.

The second, he was lucky to get away from alive. First of all, Lynette was, like, twenty-eight, a tad young for Dad. I think she worked in a casino. Her favorite drink was whiskey and soda. She dressed like a, well, I'm not going to say it, but you get the picture. And she had this annoying kid. He ran in circles around the coffee table until I thought Dad would spaz. In other words, she didn't have a thing in common with Mom.

The thing is, and Dad didn't get this — although I did right away and I told him so — she didn't want to be a partner, she wanted to be treated like his special little girl. A position, I might add, that was already taken. How did I know? Just let me say, women know women.

She wanted to go to this restaurant and that movie. She only drank this type of wine and hated Dad's chili. She couldn't stand his blues CDs and refused to walk if they could drive. She whined and whined and whined, and being in sort of a vulnerable mood, Dad always gave in.

Now, Dad has, or I should say, had, this little MG sports car which had been in our garage all of my life. At least once a week, he'd be out there in the garage, whistling away, while he just puttered around, polishing it. On sunny days he'd take Mom or me for rides along lower Marine Drive. With a big smile on his face, and the smell of the sea in our hair, we'd swing through the forest, past the glittering ships until we reached Horseshoe Bay. Then we'd eat fish and chips at Troll's while we watched the ferries come in.

Mom never drove the MG. Once, when Dad was away, I suggested we take it out. She said she'd rather not. She said it wasn't that she didn't want to drive it, or, for that matter, that Dad didn't want her to drive it, but because it was Dad's and there were very few things that he could call his own. This would always be one of them.

Like I said, Lynette didn't think the same as Mom. The day she creamed it, all she was going to do was zip around the corner for some cigarettes. Five minutes at the most. Maybe ten. Until that point, Dad had nicely refused her. Yeah, she had her own car with her, but she just really wanted to give it a try. Please, please, please?

I saw Dad's face twitch with doubt. "Alright," he finally said in this tired voice he uses with me sometimes.

I wanted to jump in and stop her. Dad's look told me: don't. So while we watched her kid race round and round and round the table, she backed out of the garage and took off down the road with a familiar buzz.

The call came half an hour later. The pickup truck hadn't seen her. The passenger's side was crushed and the front axle broken. I thought Dad might cry on the spot. He didn't, but went to get her, while I told her hyper kid to sit.

"I don't have to do what you say. You're not my mom!"

"Maybe not," I said, and I waved a threatening finger, "but you move and you're dead."

Okay, a little harsh, I admit. But I was truly fed up.

After all Dad's been through, he probably could have handled it. But it was her attitude that sucked. She didn't have the least bit of guilt.

He didn't say a word when he walked in the door. He went straight to the bathroom, while she paced back and forth, breathing hard, smoking a cigarette. Finally, Dad came out.

"You're mad at me," she said.

"I am not mad at you," he answered, in this very soft voice.

"Yes, you are. I can hear it in your voice. You're mad. Look, he didn't see me coming. What more do you want?"

Dad sat in a chair. I noticed it wasn't his favorite. He drummed his fingers impatiently against the arms. "I am not mad at you. I simply am a little shaken up."

Lynette did not believe him. "Look. Could I help it that he didn't see me? Could I help it that you drive a car no one can see?"

Dad, who was beginning to simmer, worked hard to hang back.

"Who in their right mind would want to drive a car that small!"

"You did!" Dad finally slammed back. That was it; now on his feet, he'd put up with enough.

The kid started screaming. I tried to control him, but the little creep bit me on the hand. Before I could stop him, he charged at Dad. He pounded on his legs. "Don't you yell at my mom! Don't touch her! Leave her alone, you jerk!"

Looking suddenly puzzled, Dad caught him by the arms. He looked at Lynette, then over at me. I stood rubbing my hand. This was all too foreign to him. We had never been a fighting family and I don't think he understood how quickly it had come to this. And to be honest, neither did I.

"I wasn't hurting her," he said in this deadly calm voice. He led the kid to Lynette by the hand. "I think you should go."

And she did.

Leaning with one arm against the door, Dad looked so broken I could hardly say I told you so. Instead, I started to snivel.

He put his arm around me. "It's okay, Pam. It was only a car. Let me take a look at your hand."

So, here I sit at the dinner table. Dad made this massive pot of chili, a decent mango salad and, wearing his "I love to cook" apron, served it all with some soft, doughy bread. Necessity has turned him into a passable cook.

Jennifer Reid sits across from me, blowing daintily

on her chili. *Phh*. She's wearing one of those technical suits. Powder blue, with the big white bow of her blouse wrenched around her neck in this sadistic knot. I feel like I'm strangling just looking at it. I pull at the neck-line of my sweater.

"It is such a pleasure to meet you, Pam." *Phh, Phh.* "And you're such a big girl. Your dad says you're four-teen." *Phh, phh, phh.* "And when is your birthday?"

Big girl? My birthday? Oh, pleeease, Ms. Reid, you're kidding, right? I mean, that was a joke. I look at Dad. Is she for real? Dad is smirking behind his serviette.

"November 15th." Then I add, in this casual voice, "And when is yours?"

My question catches her off guard, so that she for-gets to *phh* and burns her tongue. I smile at Dad. He scowls back.

"Oh, it's a month from today. June 26th."

"And how old will you be?"

"Pamela — have another piece of bread." Dad shoves the bread basket in my face. "And stuff it in your mouth."

"No thanks, Dad." I smile sweetly.

"Oh, that's alright, Ken. I'll be forty. Sort of a big one. You know, lordy, lordy, guess who's forty?" She kind of giggles.

She's real cool, Dad. Real cool. You picked a co-median. Lordy, lordy. Look who's forty. Kind of, like, it's all downhill from here ... one foot on the banana peel ...

"You mean, like, you're not getting older, you're just getting better?"

This time, Dad's look is accompanied with a firm foot applied to my shin under the table.

Hey! It's a lot better than what I was thinking.

Jennifer clears her throat. "Something like that."

It's pretty quiet for a while. Just the sounds of *phh, phh* and spoons clanking and Jennifer's tidy little burp. Pat, pat with the napkin. "Do you like your teacher, Pamela?"

Teacher? You mean the one I present a polished apple to every morning? Or do you mean orator-slash-dance-meister Mr. Bartell? Or, there's Wally the Whiz, who can work through a quadratic equation in thirty seconds, yet can't think to remember to zip up his fly. Or Ms. Lazarenko, dubbed the round mound of sound, who leads the choir from a chair.

"I have more than one."

"Of course."

Dad pours another splash of wine. Careful, Dad, you might cause her embarrassment. She might loosen that tourniquet around her stiff white neck. Dad tries to introduce something we might actually be able to discuss.

"You might be interested in this, Jenn. Pamela likes to bead bracelets and belts and — " Dad kind of looks to me for assistance. "What else, dear?" Because, as he suddenly realizes, he's never paid much attention to that kind of stuff. So as not to embarrass him, I kindly help out.

"I've done some blouses and purses — oh, and I beaded a cat collar once. For Nana Jean's Prince."

Having done his part, Dad sits comfortably back. Until Jennifer Reid answers with an unenthusiastic, "Oh, isn't that swell."

Swell? Swell?? What prehistoric language is that?!

Well, anyway, Dad tried. But it doesn't surprise me that that attempt fizzled out. I had her pegged for the non-handicraft type. We scrape the bottom of our bowls, once again to the tune of uneasy silence.

I now know why Jennifer Reid is sliding into her fortieth year unmarried. The woman is a major drip. A geek. Therein lies her problem.

After a while, Dad practically shouts, "Dessert?"

"What is it?" I ask.

"Tiramisu," Dad cheerfully announces. "Jenn made it."

Jennifer Reid does that silly giggle thing again, "I wish I had, Ken. But I have to fess up. I bought it."

Like, no duh. Wait a minute. Fess up? I've got to get out of here in case that language is contagious.

"I think I'll pass," I say, standing up.

Jennifer Reid gets this hurt sort of look, so Dad frowns at me.

"I've got homework. I've got to read half a book." Which was not true. It was more like the entire book.

Let's just say, I got a bit behind.

A little while later, just as I'm about to start chapter three, there is a knock at my door. Jennifer Reid comes in to apologize.

"For what?" I have to ask. "I was the one that didn't eat your dessert."

"For asking you stupid questions."

Well, okay, I couldn't argue with that. But I had considered the source. She then sits down on the end of my bed. "May I sit down?"

"Go ahead." I mean, since you already are.

"You see, Pam — "

I could tell this was big. Whatever was coming, was a definite problem.

"I'm not very good with kids. I mean — well, I never was. The fact is, I had trouble talking to fourteen-year-olds when I was fourteen."

Oh, really? Maybe because you said words like "swell" and "fess up."

"Actually, I had very few friends. Well, that is, no friends. The other kids thought I was a little strange."

"Why's that?" I ask. I mean, since she's doing the talking.

"Probably, my interests. They were so different from the norm. For one, I loved to work through problems."

"Problems?"

"Yeah, math problems. I love numbers. There are so many things you can do with them. I could spend hour upon hour sitting in my room, solving puzzles with them. And I was good at it."

And I could tell by her rising voice that she was. This was interesting. Jennifer Reid went on for a while longer about how lonely she sometimes got when she was a kid and how she thought she was the only one in the world that had such a weird interest and how that made her weird. So, I told her that's exactly the way I feel sometimes. You know, just to make her feel better. She asked me about my baby-food jars filled with dirt and stuff and asked to see what I had beaded. She looked very carefully at the patterns. This got her going about how much fun it would be to figure them out. Then she asked if I would go shopping with her on Saturday.

"Your dad has invited me to have dinner with you at your Grandma Jean's on Sunday. It's important to me to look nice, Pam. I'm not very good at choosing clothes."

Really? I'm shocked.

"I usually leave it to the saleswomen. Would you help me pick out something less conservative? Something, perhaps trendy?"

Well, trendy might be going overboard. Let's try for fashionable to start.

"Sure, Jenn," I said. "If you like."

Well, what could I say? Clearly, she's reaching out for help.

FIVE

May 27th

It is after lunch and Joanne and Mandeep and I are standing around in the hallway. We are talking about the little girl who went missing yesterday in Lynn Canyon Park. Krissy Marshall was on a field trip with her grade two class Tuesday morning when, at some point, she disappeared. Her picture was on the news last night and in the newspaper this morning. A cute little girl, with curly blond hair and big blue eyes. She was last seen wearing blue jeans and a white blouse, and carrying a pink sweater. Like I said previously, this is not the first time someone's gone missing on one of these mountains. An entire plane went down on Mount Seymour that wasn't found for fifty years.

Tony Lasserman and John Robbel are already making plans to search for her body after school. Mike Ortega figures a cougar probably got her, and it won't be a body they're after, but a few bones. Danny Kim says the vultures would have carried off anything the cougar didn't devour. They'll be lucky to find a scrap of her clothes. They've all got their theories, but I just feel ripped off. Because now Ninety Foot will be jammed with search-and-rescue teams and I won't have it to myself. Okay, that's morbidly selfish, I know.

Sarah McMurtry walks by us. She is trying to look casual on these major shoes. The heels are like mega-building blocks and nineteen miles high. She leans forward to balance on them. Joanne, who can't stand her, because Sarah can't stand me, because I cut her Barbie doll's hair, suggests I spin my pop can in front of her so we can watch her fall down. I give it some thought. It would be hysterically funny. But in the end, I decide it's not nice.

I turn away from Sarah and back to our circle, when who walks straight up to me — and I mean directly up to me — but Danielle Higgins' new boyfriend. The one with the wicked grin. The grin he just now flashes at me. The one that is causing my throat to freeze and my heart to fail. The one that — I think he has said something. But I am very close to a major coronary, so I don't hear what it is.

"Pardon?"

"I said, hi."

"Oh," I say. Joanne jams her skinny elbow in my ribs. "Hi."

"Do you think you could help me?"

Help you? Help you? Wicked Grin — I would die for you. I would wash your clothes, cook your meals and take out your garbage for you. I'd wear black lace and scamper down the hall with your books on a silver tray for you. I'd —

I get that elbow in my ribs again. "Sure," I say.

"Which way is the gym?"

"That way," and not taking my eyes away from his, I point my arm in the wrong direction. Mandeep guides it the correct way.

He laughs. "Thanks." But before he leaves — and I'm not making this up — he glints at me.

"Glinted at you?" repeat Joanne and Mandeep when I tell them, after he walks away.

"Yes. I saw it. He glinted."

"Hmm. Anyway," says Joanne, "name's Matt Leighton. He's in grade eleven at Argyle. He plays bass and works at the Westview Safeway on Saturdays. He lives with his dad and one brother and a dog named Swat. He's been going with Danielle for about three weeks, although what started as a sweet relationship appears to be turning sour. They've been seen arguing up at the

Center, and Friday left Linda Yip's party separately."

Mandeep and I are staring at her with our mouths open. "How do you know all this?"

Joanne shrugs. "I've made it a point to find out."

The most embarrassing event of my life took place after lunch today. Okay, like, I know I said dancing with Mr. Bartell was, but that was like nothing, compared to this.

Like I said, it was after lunch. I was sitting in English class, just minding my own business, thinking pleasant thoughts about Matt Leighton. When suddenly, Mr. Bartell started to bellow. He was backing up some kind of lame point by reading from *Lord of the Flies*. Knowing how I would likely be the first one to be asked a question, I reluctantly set Matt aside. And I listened. He was building up to the part about the death of Piggy —

"Piggy, saying nothing, with no time for even a grunt, traveled through the air sideways from the rock, turning over as he went. The rock bounded twice and was lost in the forest."

Mr. Bartell's voice became more daunting,

"Piggy fell forty feet and landed on his back across that square, red rock in the sea."

His emphasis was — on — every — word.

"His head opened and stuff came out and turned red. Piggy's arms and legs twitched a bit, like a pig's —"

Mr. Bartell stopped — and listened. There was a new noise in the room. With this inquisitive look, he glanced around trying to find it. I couldn't help it. I just started bawling. Something just hit me and that was it. But he didn't notice the noise was coming from me. He continued,

"Like a pig's after it has been killed. Then the sea —"

I was wailing louder than even Mr. Bartell could yell now. I don't know what happened. I just lost it. The tears were coming so hard and fast, I couldn't even breathe. And I couldn't get a word out to tell them that, really, I was alright. Really, I was. I was just — having a moment. It was just — just — I don't know. I went on bawling. There was this confused silence all around me. Mr. Bartell scratched his scrawny beard and glanced nervously down at his book.

"Oh, no," I heard him say through my splutters. "How ignorant of me."

By this time, both Joanne and Mandeep were on either side of me.

"I'm very sorry, Pamela," said Mr. Bartell. "That

was thoughtless of me. Girls, help Pamela down to Mrs. Dalrymple's office."

Following his orders, Joanne and Mandeep helped me stand up. They steered me past the staring eyes, down the hall and into Mrs. Dalrymple's office. After they left, I continued to snivel and snort, while trying to convince Mrs. Dalrymple I was quite alright. She had a suggestion.

"Perhaps, Pamela, you would like to study another book. I'm sure Mr. Bartell would agree to it. Something with a little less — violence."

Oh, wouldn't that be sweet. Special Pam studying *Anne of Green Gables* because she was far too delicate to handle anything with a spot of blood.

His head opened and stuff came out and turned red.

No one believes it, but I can take it. It doesn't bother me. Really, it doesn't. That's not the problem. I —

Yes, that is the problem. That's the only problem. I want my mom back. I want her to knock at my bedroom door and come walking in. I want her to bring me my folded laundry. I want her to tell me to get my homework done. I want her to show me the wool she picked out for my Christmas sweater. I want to go with her for a walk in the canyon, up the old logging trails, where every step on the thick forest floor is a new adventure. Like we did, before April. I want her all in one piece, together, with Dad and I again. Sometimes,

I get so, so mad at her for doing this to me. And at Dad, for letting it happen. I want this sadness that's been part of me since she died to go away. It's like this mean little animal deep inside me. Munching at my guts. Feeding on me day after day after day after day. Once in a while taking a great vicious chomp. It hurts so much sometimes, it's just about more than I can take. Like today.

There is a painting by Emily Carr called "Mountain Forest." In my heart, I know where it is. It's somewhere in British Columbia's coastal mountains. It's somewhere in Lynn Canyon. It's somewhere off a logging trail high up Lynn Peak. I love that painting. I love it because Mom is in it. Mom and April. A thousand billion words could not begin to describe it, but I will try.

The mountains form the background. They appear so, like, ancient and eternal. In the foreground these centuries-old Douglas fir soar up from the blackness of the forest to a pale sky. And all around them, the younger growth is chaotic. Rich and green and blue and purple. And at the very bottom of the painting, I see a tiny graveyard. When you look at it, there is something about that graveyard that is as comfortable and certain as the mountain. Perhaps it's just that the rock is the same color. Perhaps because a mountain and a graveyard are forever. But that is where I see Mom and April.

I'm going to visit them soon. I'm going to trek up the logging trails and sit and look over those mountains. Of course, the graveyard won't really be there. But Mom and April will. They will forever be there, forging the pillars of those mountains. They will forever be there, nudging the buds of young growth. I'm going to go soon. I'm going to go when I am ready.

My dad never will. My dad will never set foot in Lynn Canyon Park again. That is his decision. But I cannot get away from it. It is a major part of me. Mom made it that way.

SIX

I am following Joanne down the path to Ninety Foot after school. I don't want to be here (which I told her), but she insisted I come. She plans to casually bump into Tony Lasserman, who she knows will be down here in the canyon searching for Krissy Marshall. She's suddenly got this thing for him and she needs me for some kind of support.

"Come on, Pam," she'd said to me after the final bell rang. Elbowing in front of me, she'd slammed my locker door shut. "It would be *too* obvious if I'm all by myself."

"But I don't want to go down there while everyone's searching. I don't think it's right for us to be hanging around. It's not like it's a party or something."

"*Please*. I'd do it for you."

I'd looked at her big eyes all full of Tony Lasserman. One thing about Joanne is, she doesn't give up easily. The thing about me is, I do. "Oh, alright," I'd reluctantly agreed.

So far, we've jumped about three dozen monster slugs driven out into the open by the rain. And we've bumped into about a million people. They are mostly dressed in yellow hooded raincoats and black rubber boots. They are tromping through the thick foliage, stirring up the smell of cedar. They are plodding into tangled places where hardly anyone ever goes. As you can imagine, the mood down here is real grim. In fact, the only ones appearing to enjoy themselves in all this mass hysteria are John Robbel and Tony Lasserman. Joanne and I find them down by Ninety Foot, laughing coarsely, jabbing beneath the ferns with big sticks, kicking at clumps of moss.

"You're wasting your time. You'll never find her," Joanne tells Tony, nimbly striking up a conversation. "No one will." Her voice kind of lingers after she has spoken, echoing off the granite walls.

Tony continues to prod at a mass of sticks and moss caught in the bank by the creek. He removes a beer can with the tip of his stick and hucks it across the water. It clangs loudly against the rock on the other side. "Somebody's going to."

"Maybe. Ten years from now when they're out walking their dog. There'll be a tiny story next to the obits. The headline will read, 'Bones Identified As Girl Who Went Missing Ten Years Ago.'"

Tony prods for another few seconds, then leans on his stick and looks at Joanne. "Yeah, you're probably right." He draws his hand through the air and kind of laughs, "'Dental Records Confirm It. Only her dentist knew for sure. She had Dracula teeth.'"

I think it's kind of lame, not to mention morbid, but Joanne laughs out loud. But then, it doesn't really matter what *she* thinks. Because she's in love. I don't quite get this thing she's developed for Tony lately. I mean, he's alright, I guess. He's no Jason Priestly in the looks department, but he does have this big overwhelming laugh. Joanne likes that. So now she stands looking at him. And because she liked his joke so much, he stands looking at her. Like it's the first time they've noticed each other, even though for three years now, they've been in the same class. Half a minute passes and still neither of them says anything. It's like some invisible cupid somewhere has pressed a button and put them on pause, while they sort through their confusing thoughts.

Oh, Tony! Oh, Joanne! How could I have been so blind! Here I've been searching all of my life, when all along, you were the one! Crash.

I don't know about you, but I get very uncomfortable in these situations. Not only that, it's real boring for the not-involved. I watch a gull glide high above me. I know it's a young one; his belly is still gray. He lands by the creek about twenty yards down. I shuffle my feet. "Uh-humm." Excuse me. I know sparks are flying here, but can life as we know it continue on?

Sometimes I could strangle Joanne for the predicaments she puts me in. Like, what am I supposed to do here? Make some excuse like suddenly I've got this real pressing appointment or something? Or am I supposed to act like their moderator? You know, try to get conversation going because they're both so lovestruck they've forgotten how to talk? Whatever. Right now, all I want to do is say something — anything — just to relieve the extreme tenseness of the situation. So guys, looks like it might rain again tomorrow. What do you think? Or how about — Hey, Tony, what about those Grizzlies? But I know if I do, my voice will streak through the air like an annoying bug. So I guess I'll keep standing here, as still as a tree trunk. John Robbel is safe, whacking at bushes a little way down the river. Actually, this is rare. It's not often I see Joanne stuck for words.

"So," Joanne finally drawls.

I breathe a sigh of relief. There's life in them!

"How'd you do on the math test?"

Oh, major groan, Jo. That's too pathetic. Math test? Who do you think you are? His mom?

Tony shrugs and throws his stick away. "I could have done better. Probably should have studied. Wally's been making them tougher than he used to." He walks over and stands in front of Joanne. Close.

Now's my chance. I start to back away. But Joanne snatches my shirt and forces me to stay put. Like something enormous is about to happen. So, I do.

"Hey, Joanne," Tony begins, "I was wondering. Would you maybe want to do something with me sometime?"

Joanne crosses her arms, shifts her feet and, now that she's got his interest, tries to play it real coy. "Oh yeah? Something like what?"

"I don't know. Like go to a movie or the mall or something. Or — hey, are you going to Ortega's grad party?"

"Yeah, I was going to go with Pam."

He looks at me quickly, like I'm this irritation or something. Don't mind me. I don't want to go anyway.

"Yeah? Well, maybe we can all go together. You know, you and me, and John and her?"

Her? The name's not her, buddy. It's me! Pamela. Got it?

Joanne doesn't even look at me when she agrees. "Sure. We could do that."

Wait a minute. We? How did I get dragged into this? Oh sure, it's okay for you two. You seem to have something going on here. But what do I have in common with John Robbel? I look over at him. He's using his stick as a spear to scare away my gull. He misses.

He wipes his nose with the back of his hand and tries again. Real classy, you bird killer. Lucky "her."

See, Joanne has this problem about fixing me up with guys. In fact, my first disgusting kiss was set up by her. It was in grade seven and took place at one of her parties. It was with Landon Farquharson, who I sort of liked and I guess sort of liked me. Anyway, Joanne figured we should celebrate our like for each other with a kiss. The very reason she arranged the party. She had asked Landon ahead of time if he wanted to kiss me. He must have said it could be alright. Then she asked me if I would mind. I think I said something like, I guess not.

Mostly we just sat around the basement, talking, listening to music, eating chips and Cheezies and Nuts' n' Bolts. Joanne's mother came down once in a while to refill the bowls. One time, after she'd left, Joanne winked at me. She turned the lights real low. This was the agreed-upon signal. I looked at Landon who was sitting next to me. He turned to me. In the dim light his big face came down, looming closer and closer. But all I could see was the Cheezie dust all over his lips. He pressed them against mine. We stayed stuck together like that for what seemed an eternity. Luckily, Joanne's mother came winging down the stairs again looking for something she'd forgotten. She flicked on all the lights and pushed games at us, like Pictionary and Balderdash and stuff. I was so glad it was over I could have jumped up and kissed *her*. For the next two days, I couldn't get the taste of Cheezies out of my mouth. I guess my moral here, or whatever, is don't stuff your face just before you kiss.

"Okay," Tony says. "Why don't we figure to go about eight. I'll tell John to pick Pam up. We'll all meet at your house."

"Pam doesn't need to be picked up," I say. "I can get there by myself."

They give me this surprised look, like they've suddenly noticed I'm a living human being or something. Not only that, I can talk.

"So — it's okay with you?" Joanne asks.

"I guess," I shrug.

SEVEN

May 28th

Danny Kim totally lost it in the library today. It was right after lunch. He came walking in, wearing these plastic glasses with giant bloodshot eyeballs that hung out on springs. With this crazy laugh, he jumped up on a table. Then, leaping from one table to the next, he made these sorry attempts to crack jokes. Saying stuff like, "Nice ring, let me have a closer look," and "Here's looking at you, kid." This was Mr. Ninety-Nine Point Nine Percent, Danny. Mr. Class President for the last three years. Mr. Winner of the Debate Club, acting so bizarre, it was pathetic.

The major problem here is, you don't talk in our

school library. You don't eat, drink, turn pages or push out chairs too noisily in our library. Whispering is pounced on and giggling is practically a capital offence. So when Mrs. Zimmerman, the librarian, came walking out of the back room pushing a cart of books and Danny was standing on our table, laughing stupidly, and we were trying to tell him to get a grip, she went ballistic.

"Danny Kim! Just what do you think you're doing?"

"Hey, Mrs. Z! Want to dance?" Danny did a little jig on our table. "I've got my party eyes on."

"Get down! I want to speak to you right now! And that goes for everyone at your table!"

Joanne, Mandeep, Linda Yip and I looked at one another. We started to protest.

"But we weren't doing any — "

"Now!"

By Mrs. Z's hostile tone, it was apparent we didn't have a hope. So, following Danny, we filed quietly into her office. She closed the door behind us. For several moments, she didn't say a thing. She just stood there with her arms folded and this real intense look on her face. She stuck an upturned hand toward Danny. He gave her the glasses.

"Now, what is the meaning of all this?"

Danny's face lost all trace of humor. It was now the reverse. He looked so sad and so lost, I thought he was going to cry. "I was just trying to have some fun," he told her.

Mrs. Z adjusted her glasses and glowered. At Danny, at Joanne, at Mandeep, at Linda and at me. "Trying to have some fun?" she repeated dryly.

"Yes," Danny practically whimpered. "I guess it's not allowed."

Mrs. Z pressed her lips together, forming a hard white line. She unfolded her arms and planted them on her hips. "Well, Mr. Kim, you guess right. That kind of — fun," she sucked the word like it had a sour taste, "is *not* allowed. The library is a place for quiet study and intellectual enjoyment. It is not a place for twisted entertainment."

"I know, but, you don't understand — "

"What is it about what I have just said that *you* don't understand?"

"I wasn't trying — "

"Mr. Kim, if you were a weak student studying for an exam — an exam that could make the difference between passing and failing the year — and you were prevented from doing so by the inappropriate behavior of one very loud student — what would you call that?"

Danny lifted his eyes from the floor. He looked helplessly over at me. I mouthed the word rude.

"What was that?"

"Rude?" whispered Danny.

"Rude indeed! Not to mention inconsiderate and disrespectful! Would you be tolerant of a student like that?"

"I guess not."

"What was that?"

"No."

"You wouldn't?"

"NO!"

Danny's thunderous response compelled Mrs. Z to silence. But it was only temporary. "Of course, you wouldn't." With these needle eyes, she slowly studied each one of our faces. "Now, I hope I have helped you ALL understand we have rules for a reason. They were not drawn up simply to amuse me and Mrs. Lofts. You must also understand that, when student behavior is inconsistent with these rules, action must be taken. By doing this, we are attempting to teach you responsibility. Responsibility to yourself and to those around you. With that in mind, you are all suspended from the library for one week."

With this shocked expression, Danny looked up from the floor and at all of us. "But Mrs. Z! It had nothing to do with them!"

Shh, Danny. Shh. Holding my finger to my lips, I shook my head. Never mind. She'll really blow.

"Mr. Kim! As far as I'm concerned, it had everything to do with them! An enthusiastic audience is as much a part of the play as the actor! Now, all of you, off to your next class!"

I was right. She blew. We all slunk out.

You might think we would be mad at Danny. But

we weren't. We felt sorry for him. We knew why he did it. Something Mrs. Z didn't know. Or if she did, she didn't care. We knew his brother, Wilson, had run away from home. Wilson was seventeen, three years older than Danny. He'd been to school off and on through junior high, but since he'd turned sixteen, not at all. Wilson had done some pretty manic things in his life-time. Like fed the hose through their neighbor's window when they were gone for a weekend. And turned it on. Set his bedroom on fire when he was mad at his mom. Tied Danny to a tree in the Canyon because he did so well in school. And left him there. Crashed Darla Miller's party and annihilated her dad's wine collection.

Now he was charged with assault and theft. Which was the reason he had run away. Wilson and a friend had knocked two kids to the ground, roughed them up and stolen their bikes. The police found the mangled frames four days later in the Capilano River.

Danny's parents fretted day and night over Wilson. First it was maybe if they put him in basketball, he would get along better with the other kids. Then, maybe if he went to private school, he would get better marks. Maybe if they bought him designer clothes, he would have more self-esteem. Maybe if they bought him a computer, he'd develop an interest. Maybe a car would get him away from his friends in Lynn Valley. Maybe, if they took him to Paris, the cat-poisoning incident would blow over. Maybe, maybe, maybe. Yes, Danny? Oh, ninety-nine-point-nine percent is good. Very good, dear. But what about your brother, Willie? Maybe if we take him to Bishop's for his birthday, just the three of us, he would appreciate what we do for him. Your birthday, Danny? Oh sure, you can have a couple of kids over for pizza. But we'll be going out.

Danny couldn't compete. No matter what he did, or how well he did it, Wilson always had one up on him. All Danny really wanted was to be noticed. Today, Mrs. Z noticed him.

I was making Hamburger Helper for Dad and me when he got the call. I knew it was Mrs. Z, because Dad said hello, then was quiet while he looked over at me. Frowning.

He continued frowning, in silence, for some time. "Thank you for calling, Mrs. Zimmerman. It will be dealt with," was all that he said.

Dealt with? What's there to deal with?

"Dad, look, I can explain," I said, before Dad had even hung up. "Danny snapped and we were just trying to calm him down."

"By disturbing everyone in the library? By preventing the serious students from getting their work done? Don't you think that's just a little bit — "

"Rude?" I said, jumping right in. "Yes, definitely. It would be rude, inconsiderate and disrespectful. If it were the case. But like I said, we were only trying to help Danny."

"Couldn't you have picked a more thoughtful way? For instance, one in keeping with library rules?"

I knew Dad wasn't really as mad as he was pretending. Mrs. Z had got him all hyped up. She made him believe it was his parental duty to harass me. I also knew what Dad really thought of people like Mrs. Z. By the book. No exceptions. No time to listen to excuses. I'd seen Dad's picture from high school. Just his long hair told me he wasn't exactly the conformist type. I couldn't help just a tiny smile.

Dad tried to disguise his own. "What do you mean, Danny snapped?"

So I told him about Wilson's latest crime. About what an embarrassment he is to Danny. How at home, Danny is always ignored in favor of Wilson. How unfair it is and that I wished Wilson would never come back.

Dad agreed that it wasn't fair. But then, life often isn't fair. Something I'd heard him say mega-times before. "You can't change the world, Pam. All you can do is offer Danny your support."

Lifting two plates from the cupboard, I spooned out the Hamburger Helper.

"Still," Dad said, as I set it before him. "I can't let this go unnoticed. I told her I'd deal with it."

We thought about this as we ate.

"You could ground me," I suggested.

"Okay. How about Sunday night? That still leaves your weekend open."

Thoughtful of him, but, "Aren't we going to Nana's Sunday night?"

"Oh, right. I forgot. Hmm. Monday then?"

I considered it. "Yeah. I can't see why not."

"Good. Monday it is." Dad seemed relieved. We finished our supper. Dad stretched as he stood up. "And since we'll be at home, why don't you ask Danny for dinner?"

"Okay. And maybe Mandeep?"

Dad nodded.

EIGHT

May 29th

Danielle Higgins is lucky she's got a perfect body. Because other than that, she's nothing but a creep. She is rude. She's insulting. And if there's something she wants, she'll crush and grind anybody that gets in her way. That includes our teachers.

It's like she doesn't have a conscience. Like she figures the whole world is hers for the taking and all the rest of us should serve it up for her on our bended knees. And if we refuse, well, we just better watch out. I guess I'm lucky. She's never made me a target. She's always looked right past me, or through me. I've never been any kind of threat. Like, no duh.

Not that she has to have a particular thing against you. Sometimes she'll pick on someone for no reason. Usually, just because she's bored. It's been Danny Kim this week. Nothing too direct, just these nasty little digs. Like when Wally gave us a math sheet, then left the room for a few minutes this morning, Danielle took one look at it and made this spluttery sound with her lips. No doubt, it was a bit beyond her. Bored, needing entertainment, she began to look around, chomping her gum, slapping her pencil eraser against her desk. Her eyes fell on Danny.

"Hey, Danny?"

Danny, who was already half finished, looked up through a blur. "Huh?"

"Is your dad out of work?"

He blinked. "What? No. Why are you asking me that?"

"Just wondering," Danielle shrugged. She pretended to rediscover her worksheet.

"Why did you ask me that?"

Pretty well the entire class was looking at her now. We all wanted to know.

Danielle didn't look up. "Oh, just the fact that your family couldn't afford a new bike for your brother. Made me think money in the Kim house must be tight."

If it had been anyone else who had said it, nobody would have laughed. But because it was Danielle, half the class, all the boys, did laugh. It was beside the point whether they thought it was funny or not. It was the sexy Danielle who had spoken.

I could see Danny wanted to club her, but he's far too dignified for that. He went back to his worksheet.

Danielle also plays teachers against one another. Like when she's trying to bump up a mark. Like when she barely made sense on a social studies essay and brought it to the attention of Mr. Overhand.

"But Mr. O, I don't understand." A flutter of her lashes. "On my last English essay, I got ninety-five percent. Mr. Bartell wrote comments like 'fresh' and 'distinctive.' I was only trying to refine my style."

So, guess what? Smitten with self-doubt, Mr. O bumped her up fifteen percent.

Then there was the time she was just plain mean to Mrs. Lazarenko, our amazingly obese music teacher who conducts the choir from a chair. Danielle was determined that for one class, she was going to make her stand up. So she spread tacks, points up, on her chair. Mrs. Lazarenko came waddling in as usual, opened a music book on the piano, struck a note, repeated it in voice and, as we waited for a reaction, settled into her chair.

There was no reaction.

"Alright class, 'California Dreamin',' once through, beginning now," and she bellowed the first few words.

Our mouths hung open, but no sound came out.

She stopped short. "Are you with me, class? Or is it up to me to give a solo performance?" She wriggled to sit up. The white flesh hanging from her arms rippled with the effort. She began the song again.

Still our mouths hung open.

"Come on, come on."

One by one, we sort of joined in. So that we were all more or less singing when the song came to an end.

"That was terrible. Just terrible. Let's try to put a little more pizzazz in it. Come on, Joanne. Darla, heads up! Pamela, Mandeep, Danielle, look sharp!"

Mrs. Lazarenko sat on those tacks for the entire music class. When the bell went, she stood up. She shuffled back to the piano to collect her music books. And there were the tacks, embedded in her great wide butt. She bent to pick up her music. She knocked it to the floor. With great effort, she bent all the way down. One by one, like bits of ammunition, those tacks sprang out. Mrs. Lazarenko must have been wearing one major girdle. Like large enough to cover the state of Montana. Ping, ping, ping. We took off out of the classroom to avoid being struck.

One of Danielle's worst stunts was what she did to Joanne. Joanne didn't tell me the whole story until yesterday. But it was the reason Joanne returned to uncool. This all happened last December.

Joanne's parents had been friends with their neighbors, the Adlers, forever it seemed. Joanne's mom and Mrs. Adler were leaders of our Girl Guide troop and played tennis in the park. Mr. Robertson and Mr. Adler helped each other in their yards in the summer. On Saturdays they'd carry lumber or fix fences or sometimes just sit out front in lawn chairs and share a beer together. And at the beginning of May, since I can remember, the Adlers and the Robertsons organized a barbecue for the entire block. I always got to stay overnight at Joanne's when it happened. We'd eat Maui ribs and blintzes stuffed with cheese until we looked like them. We'd dance in the street until long after dark, then we'd all roast marshmallows in the Adlers' backyard.

The thing I haven't mentioned yet is that the Adlers' have a son. His name is Steve and he's sixteen. He was and is really, really, good looking. Picture Leonardo DiCaprio with black hair. Anyway, Joanne and I had been drooling over him for quite a long time. Hey, he was so far out of our reach, it was allowed. We've always been just noisy little kids to him.

Oh, for this to make sense, you have to know that the Adlers are Jewish.

So, what happened is, last November when Joanne was cool, she went to this party with Danielle. It was with a bunch of people from senior high. And who should she meet there but her neighbor, Steve Adler. He didn't even recognize Joanne at first. Not now that she had turned fourteen. Not in her cool all-grown-up state. But as Joanne said, he must have liked what he saw because he hung around her most of the evening. He called her the next day. They went to a movie together and for a bite to eat at the mall. Everything was going real smooth between them – until Danielle stepped in.

The problem was, Danielle also had this thing for Steve going on. But instead of saying anything to Joanne, she handled it in her own "distinctive" way. Joanne discovered what Danielle had done when she was helping her dad put up the Christmas lights a month later. She was in the garage getting Mr. Robertson the extra light bulbs. Mr. Robertson was carrying the ladder to the front of the house. That's when Mrs. Adler came over to talk to him. Joanne watched her cross the driveway through the garage window. Sensing some kind of weird tension in the way that Mrs. Adler walked, Joanne stayed right where she was. She just listened through the open side door. She told me the conversation went something like this:

"Hi, Debbie," her dad said. He added something about it being so sunny and warm and how he could easily get used to weather like that in December.

"I want to talk to you," Joanne imitated Mrs. Adler, in this very grave voice. "We've heard something from one of your daughter's classmates." There was then this very long pause. "We, Ben and I, know you and Susan well. At least we thought we did. And we hope what we've heard isn't true."

"Oh?" Mrs. Adler had Mr. Robertson's attention. "And what's that?"

"Your daughter — you and your family — have something against Jews."

"What?!" Joanne said her dad practically yelped. She heard a clatter like the ladder had fallen to the ground. "Where did you hear such a thing? Debbie, we've known each other a long time. I'd like to think you know us better than that."

Joanne figured that by the silence that followed, it didn't matter how long they had known each other. Or how well.

"I only know what I've heard. The things this young lady heard from Joanne are vicious. They must have come from somewhere. If our friendship has meant anything, I trust you'll put a stop to it."

"This is ridiculous," Joanne's dad continued in disbelief. "Susan and I have always emphasized respect and tolerance in raising our children. Who said such things? Come on, Debbie, don't believe some rumor when you know it isn't true."

"Do I?"

Mrs. Adler left at that point. Whether she believed the lies Danielle had invented really didn't matter. There was now this little seed of doubt. Nothing Joanne's dad could say would squash it.

There was no block party at the beginning of May

this year. The Adlers made up some excuse. Mr. Adler and Mr. Robertson no longer carry lumber or build anything, or sit and have a beer together. Mrs. Robertson and Mrs. Adler don't play tennis anymore. For a while, the Robertsons and the Adlers would nod or lift a hand to acknowledge one another. Now, Joanne says, they don't even talk.

NINE

May 30th

Today's the day I'm going shopping with Jennifer Reid.
All morning, I've been trying to think of a style that
would define her. You know, a visible expression of
who she is. I've imagined everything from retro sixties
to nineties glitz. But what continually comes to mind is
a long flannel skirt and white blouse with a cameo at
the neck and a calculator in the pocket.

She picks me up telling me how she's been looking
forward to this all week and how we're going to have
this fab day.

Ouch! I won't survive if I have to listen to this all

day. "Oh, no kidding," I say. "Fab. More than fab. Maybe even awesome." I must discreetly try to update her lingo.

We head to the Park Royal Shopping Center.

I think I've forgotten to mention something about me. I hate shopping. I know, like, my gender is supposed to be wild for it. Don't get me wrong, I like to look nice. But I can't go for hour upon hour and from store to store and stay interested. I get bored after thirty minutes. Joanne, on the other hand, could make a career of it. If she were paid to prance around stores, modeling in mirrors the way she does, she'd very quickly be a wealthy woman. And if I were paid for the number of hours I've been forced to stand there watching her, I would also make a few bucks. So, I have to admit, I was already pretty certain this day was going to be tedious.

We walk in the store, and there in front of us is a mannequin dressed in narrow black pants, silk shirt and a soft suede jacket. Too *Cosmo* for me, but for Jennifer? If she could handle leaving the collar open, it just might work. And I tell her so.

"Think so?"

"Yeah, I think so."

She tries it on.

"Alright!" I'm really quite impressed.

Jennifer buys the entire outfit, just like that. Well, that was easy. Let's see, what else? Next, I find a totally wicked, hand-embroidered, waist-length denim jacket. Jennifer tries it on.

"Go for relaxed. Take that clip out of your hair and mess it around a bit. "

Jennifer attempts to, but relaxed causes her some stress. She moves two or three pieces out of place.

"Not like that. Like this." Using my fingers as combs, I lift her blond hair high and let it fall to float around her face. "And don't do this button up. There. What do you think?"

She smiles in the mirror and nods. I can tell she is pleased. Forty-five minutes later we are out of there. Jennifer carries three new outfits. And I have four new bras. Don't ask. Let's just put it down to necessity. We've done alright. To thank me, she takes me to Earl's for lunch.

"Good," she says, after we've ordered. "We've still got the entire afternoon ahead. Now we can have some fun."

Uh-oh. I remember who I am with. Ms. Mathematics. Ms. Loves to Play with Numbers. "Does this mean a thrilling quiz in calculus?" Oops! I've said it out loud.

Jennifer giggles. "Only a dweeb would do that. No. I was thinking more like a walk around the seawall. Or ice cream at Granville Island. Or, whatever you like."

And I was thinking about the word dweeb.

"Dweeb?" I ask, "Jennifer, what exactly does that mean?"

She gets this pink kind of flush. "I don't know. Kind of like a nerd, I guess. Someone who is very boring. Usually because they are so obsessed with something they can't get away from it. That's not to say that 'something' is good or bad. But they are always thinking about it and can never relax. And when they try to, really stupid things come out of their mouth. It's their attempt to make them seem like they are having fun."

"You know a lot about dweebs."

Jennifer just nods. The waitress serves us our lunch.

"Mind if we drop by my office on the way to wherever we're going, just for five minutes?"

"Okay," I say, biting into my burger. "Where *are* we going?"

"You choose."

I think for a moment. I'll say it, because I want a reaction. "What about the Art Gallery?"

Jennifer almost chokes on a red pepper. "Really? For sure? Oh, I love to walk through the Emily Carr exhibit." Her expression quickly changes from one of excitement to this quizzical look. "You're not just saying that, Pam?"

"Why?"

She stabs at her food. "Well, because you think it's something a dweeb would like to do."

I have to laugh. "If it is, that makes me one too."

Jennifer smiles and relaxes.

"How's that stir-fry?" I ask.

"Tops!" she says. She sees my mouth drop open. "I mean tasty. Very tasty. In fact, you might even call it super. No. It's awesome. It's super awesome!"

I'm laughing, "As long as you're enjoying it."

It's a long, smooth glide up the elevator to the top of the bank and Jennifer's office. Once we have stopped, we pad out the door and down the hallway on this plush pink carpet. I look behind us. My footprints are bigger than hers are.

Jennifer's humungous polished desk faces a wall of long shiny windows. And a major view of Burrard Inlet. I can see nearly the entire North Shore from way up here. From the Lions to Seymour Mountain. I can see where Lonsdale cuts high into Grouse Mountain. The cars moving up it look like tiny toys from way up here.

Jennifer tells me to make myself comfortable at her desk, she'll only be a moment. So, I do. I lean back in her big leather chair and look around me. There is only one other person here. Marie. Jennifer introduced her as her secretary on the way in. We had to walk through her glass office to get in here. I watch Marie walk toward Jennifer. She is carrying a file folder and looking real concerned. She refers to it, while asking Jennifer a question. Jennifer glances at the file, but only for a moment. Right away, she tells Marie what to do. In this confident-sounding voice. Like she knows exactly what she's talking about. But then, I guess maybe she does. After all, she is in charge up here. She must know her stuff. Jennifer and Marie finish their conversation. With — is Marie laughing? A joke? Jennifer made a joke? Well, when you're sure of yourself, I guess anything can happen.

Her chair is so cool. It rocks. It spins. It tilts. She has a super-modern computer. And a telephone that is ringing. I look at Jennifer. I look at her secretary. I push the button that is flashing.

"Hello?" I say.

"Ms. Reid?"

"No."

There is a short hesitation. "Can I speak to Ms. Reid?" The voice of an older man sounds urgent.

I am looking at the view. At the expanse of desk before me. I feel — power! This is major control. "May I ask who's calling?" I hear my voice — hot! Sizzling with confidence. It must be catchy.

"Ben Bremnar. Please, tell her it's important."

"I'll tell her. But I know she is very busy." I hold the phone away from my ear. "Ms. Reid?" I sing. "A Mr. Ben Bremnar is on the phone for you."

Jennifer leaves the secretary's office and comes over to her desk. I hand her the phone. I lean back in the chair and cross my feet on the desk. She talks to Mr. Bremnar in this real calm voice, telling him exactly what to do. Taking charge of the urgent situation. And by her manner, I can tell it is a common thing for her to do. I could see her doing it in one of her technical suits. In this room. Reflected in those windows. Next to this desk. It would fit.

"So, you're chipper with that, Ben?"

Where *does* she get these words?

"Good. Talk to you soon." She sounds so cheery, I'm sure Mr. Bremnar is better than chipper.

I think she likes this job. I think she must be half decent at it too. People seem to value what she thinks and says. That must make her feel good.

"Okay, let's get out of here, Pam. Marie, we're off to the Art Gallery."

Marie is standing in the door to her office, smiling. "You two have a good time."

I just had a thought. Maybe I have Jenn all wrong. Maybe she isn't so weird. Maybe she's had plenty of takers. Maybe she's just been having too much fun doing what she likes to do.

Three hours later we are on our way home, driving down Ross Road in Lynn Valley, when I spot Matt Leighton. He has stopped to throw a stick for Lupus, Mr. Spinelli's German shepherd. Lupus tries to trap anyone who walks by his yard into playing with him. He's been doing it for as long as I can remember. Matt leans back, aiming so Lupus gets a good run, just short of the house. He hurls the stick. Lupus tears after it.

"Now that's a healthy-looking specimen," Jenn comments.

"Yeah. He begs to play every time you walk by the house."

Jenn looks at me with her eyes smiling. "I didn't mean the dog."

I feel my face flush. She must have seen me looking.

TEN

I've decided that I'm going to be a shiftless drifter when I grow up. With no fixed address. It's the easiest out. I am fed up with people asking me what I want to be. I can't even think about it. These last few years have been so screwy, I can hardly think ahead to the next day. Even plans for the next hour can be iffy. Six years from now? It may as well be sixty.

Mrs. Dalrymple came into homeroom yesterday to discuss course choices for next year. We should have a good idea of where we're going, she said, so we don't limit our options in the future. We have to think hard about our interests and abilities. And discuss it with our parents. And remember, the world is our oyster.

What a gross saying. It doesn't make the least bit of sense.

Some people know exactly what they want to do. Darla Miller wants to be a veterinarian. She's been big into horses since she was six years old. Mike Ortega is going to take over his dad's garage someday. He's never considered anything else. Danielle Higgins wants to be, big surprise, a supermodel. Never mind that she's only five-foot-two. Joanne is considering becoming an elementary schoolteacher, an engineer or a talk-show host.

"Is that something you just decide to be?" I asked after Mrs. Dalrymple had left the classroom. I was referring to her third choice.

"Yeah, I guess so. If the world is my oyster, I can decide whatever I want. What about you, Pam?"

"I already told you. A shiftless drifter."

"Can't," said Mandeep. "You're already over qualified. You should have dropped out in grade eight. I'm going to take fine arts and play flute with the Vancouver Symphony Orchestra. What about you, Lynn?"

"My mom wants me to be a dentist."

"Ooooo!" we all groaned.

"How could you stand to put your hands in just anyone's mouth?" I asked. "Can you imagine, like, Carl Jenkins? Or — or Mr. Bartell's?"

"Ooooooo!" we all said again, including Linda.

"I'll be so good, I can be super selective."

Joanne looked at me. "Seriously, Pam. There are so many things you are good at. Look how well you did on your English essay. What about a writer of some type?"

It was true. Mr. Bartell gave me ninety-six percent on the in-class essay we wrote on Thursday. He said I showed "incredible insight into the group dynamics of the tribes." I think he was sucking up to me for causing me to lose it in class. "I don't have any ideas," I answered. "And nobody wants to listen, if you don't have anything to say."

"Well, what about a forest ranger? Then you could spend all your time sitting up in a tree."

I made a face. "Why don't you forget the flute and become a comedian, Mandeep?"

Joanne wouldn't drop it. "You like art. You like paintings. Who's that artist you really get off on? You know, that weird one that had rodents for pets. She was a member of the Group of Seven?"

I was forced to roll my eyes. "Emily Carr. She was not a member of the Group of Seven. And she wasn't weird. You should be so weird that you can paint like that."

"Come on, Pam. Don't get so hostile. We're only trying to help."

And I guess they were. But there's this thing I can't tell them because they would never understand. A year and a half ago, I was, like, this little girl, still growing up. That ended, like, boom. And now, I'm this semi-adult who has to make these major decisions about what I'm going to do with the rest of life. The thing is, I don't want this happening. Not yet. Not now. Not without my mom knowing. But I can't make it stop. My whole world is changing, getting way out of my control. When I want it to stand still. But it's not just me. Everyone around me is changing. There's this whole major attitude change that sucks.

Like our teachers. Two years ago, they didn't act like it was a pain if we asked them questions. A few years ago, they had patience with us. Now, it seems we're too difficult to teach. Like if we open our mouths, they can't wait to get them shut.

In stores the sales clerks used to be helpful. Now, they follow us around like hawks. On the other hand, reluctantly remembering "The Peach Sweater Incident," I guess they have every right.

Then there are the other things. Like trying to get used to these gazelle legs of mine. And like my period which started. And other parts of me bugging out. Some days, I'm so sore and tender and bloated and achy. But there's no one I can tell. Not even Dad. Because I hate to say it, but he's part of all this. It's like I'll break or something if he plays with me, throws me around the way he used to. Or like he'll get a disease if he gives me a giant hug. Sometimes, I think it might be something I've done.

Boys in general have gone weird. Two years ago, they acted real stupid. But at least they ignored us.

Now, they act even more stupid, but they do it staring at our chests. I hate it. Can you imagine if we stared at them in a certain place like that? They'd be so self-conscious they'd probably duck out of the room, thinking something was majorly wrong.

I wish there was someone I could talk to. Other than Joanne and my friends. We have discussions about these things, but they don't amount to much. Like last summer, when we were tanning on my back lawn. Joanne insisted you're a woman the minute you get your first period. You're a woman because you can have a baby if you want.

"That's stupid," Linda told her. "How can my little sister be a woman? She got her period when she was eight."

Then Mandeep said, "I think Joanne is right. You're a woman when you can procreate. When it comes down to it, isn't that the reason we were put on this earth?"

"Procreate?" said Linda.

"Yeah, you know, reproduce."

Linda frowned, like she always does when our talk turns to semi-serious stuff. "Okay. Maybe. But what if you don't get your period? Say, like, for some medical reason, and you can never procreate. Does that mean you're a child your entire life?"

"Yeah, Joanne," Mandeep now agreed with Linda. "Or what about if you don't get your period, but you have a test-tube baby or whatever. So what does that make you then?"

Joanne shrugged. "Well, I guess if you're twenty or something, a woman, I guess."

"So it comes down to age?" said Mandeep.

"Legally, you're an adult when you turn eighteen." I'm not sure how I knew that.

"Pam's right. So, that's it. You're a woman when you turn eighteen." Linda settled back in the lawn chair and closed her eyes.

Mandeep looked at her watch. "Time to turn," she said, sipping her lemonade in the shade of the umbrella. She's our timekeeper when we tan, but she never tans herself. She says she's brown enough already.

The rest of us flipped to our stomachs. We were quiet for a while, letting the hot sun soak into our backs.

"I still think it's when you start your period," said Joanne.

Aside from my height and the period thing, there are a zillion other changes since Mom. My entire wardrobe is different. My hair has grown six inches and been cut twice. I've changed my room around. I made a pumpkin-pecan cake for Dad's birthday. He didn't want me to. But I had to. It's the one Mom always baked. I have a jar of sand from Ucluelet. And a peach pit from the Okanagan. And then, there's this other thing that happened, that nobody knows about. Not even Dad.

I like ice skating. Joanne and I have been going ice

skating together since we were nine years old. Every Friday night during the winter, we take the bus from the Center, down Mountain Highway to the arena at the Winter Club. At nine o'clock, we take it back. We get off at the Center again and walk all the way down Ross Road. Joanne goes into her house. And I walk farther, turning on Hoskins toward mine.

Last January was when it happened. Joanne had gone into her house. I was continuing down the street toward mine. This guy, like about eighteen or whatever, was passing me. He was walking the opposite way, on the other side of the street. I didn't look at him. I kept my eyes on the sidewalk. This is because I don't like to look in the eyes of people who I don't even know. It was dark, but it wasn't raining. Actually, it was quite warm. We passed. But then the sound of his footsteps didn't continue like they should have. I heard them stop, then swing around. They became louder again, coming after me. He was right next to my side.

I walked quicker. He walked quicker alongside me. He hung his arm over my shoulder.

"Hey, sweetie. Where are you going in such a hurry?"

His breath was bad. His long whiskers scratched against my cheek. I had never had a man — not even my dad — so close to me. I tried to run, but he threw an arm across my collarbone and slammed my back against his chest.

"Where are you going, doll?" he hissed.

I couldn't move. I was pinned against him and he was pressing his hand across my mouth. He hissed more things, worse things, in my ear. And as he said these things, he ripped a button from my jacket and he squeezed – he *kept on squeezing* – one of my breasts! I struggled hard but I couldn't move. And he kept on doing it. And it hurt so much! And I couldn't do anything! Except blubber like a little baby. Because it hurt. But mostly because I *hated* him. I hated him so much I would have killed him if I could have got my arms free. Instead, I bit him on the hand he had wrapped around my neck.

Right at that very same moment a car came around the corner, sweeping light across us. It came to a sudden stop. He let go of me and I started running, faster than I have ever run in my life. I ran and ran and ran. I could feel my heart, like it was ready to explode, just below the skin of my chest. I didn't look back. I just kept on going. I tore up our driveway and flew in the side door, down the hallway and into my bedroom. I curled in a ball and rocked back and forth on my bed. I couldn't stop crying. But I had to do it quietly. I didn't want Dad to hear me. I could hear him on the telephone in his den. I pulled my pillow over my head and nearly choked myself so he wouldn't. But it was nearly an hour before I could catch my breath. And another one before I could even think again. A little while later I came out of my room. Dad was surprised to find me sorting beads and folding scraps of fabric in Mom's hobby room. He said he was just about to call Joanne's. He was beginning to get worried. He hadn't known that I was home.

I took a long shower that night and another one the next morning. I tried to get the smell of that man out of my head. But I never could. I mean, I can't. I can still smell him. And sometimes, my breast still hurts. I wish sometimes there was someone I could talk to about it. Maybe that would help. But there isn't. My dad would absolutely freak. Besides, it's too embarrassing. Who would believe a thing like that would happen for no reason? They would probably think I made it up. So that's it. I keep it to myself.

Anyway, I don't feel like it happened to the real me, to the real Pamela Collins. Nothing has happened to her for quite some time. Sure, all these changes have taken place. Some kind of stuff has to fill the outer Pamela's days. But the real me is inside her hollowness. I'm stuck. I'm sitting alone in the dark, waiting for my mom to come home. I'm afraid to make a move without her. I'm afraid to turn on a light.

ELEVEN

May 31st, early afternoon

I am sitting down at Ninety Foot watching Mrs. Marshall crash through the woods. There is no method to her search. With her bare hands, she tears at the under-growth, hurls rocks over, rips at the junipers and flings fallen branches aside. She looks like some kind of rabid animal. Her hair is all matted, like it's in the early stages of dreadlocks. The cuts and scratches on her arms and face shriek this nasty red. She is way too thin, with these sunken cheeks and hollow black eyes. I want to tell her to go home and take a hot bath. Eat a good meal. Read a book with her two other children. The ones I see sluffing around the Center like they have no place to go.

The search team has dwindled. But she's making up for it. I see her all the time, tearing crazily at some part of the canyon. I tried to talk to her once. It's frightening. Her eyes are unseeing, like windows to some chaotic planet. She's nothing like the Mrs. Marshall I used to know. The one that taught us how to make Santa Claus ornaments during craft days in elementary school. She was so patient with Randy Carlyle, who got frustrated and began acting stupid, stuffing green embroidery thread up his nose.

I told her she looked thirsty and offered to share some of my lemonade with her.

"Can't you see I'm looking for my daughter?" she shrieked at me. "I haven't got time for that." She looked at my thermos like it held poison. And at me like how dare I interrupt her mission.

I've seen Mr. Marshall bring her food. She shoves it in. Not tasting. Still looking. Kicking the ground with her worn-out shoe. I've seen him when it's nearing dark, nudging at her, gently pulling her arm, pleading with her to come home. He tries to calm her while she cries and carries on. Finally, reluctantly, she leaves Lynn Canyon and her little daughter. But just for that night.

TWELVE

May 31st, evening

Nana Jean worries a lot. She fusses over little things and doesn't smile very much. She's always telling Dad what to do. She tells me what to do. She tells Dad's brother, Uncle Sean, what to do and his wife, Lilly, as well. She has suggestions for Aunt Andrea, Uncle Nick and all my cousins too. When we visit, she clears her throat a lot and fidgets with her rings, while her hands are folded in her lap.

She's totally unlike Grandpa was. He died of cancer when I was five. But I still remember him bouncing me on his knee, tweeking my nose, and his big thundering laugh.

I like Nana Jean. I mean, I love her, I guess. It's just that she's too critical to be fun. She's critical of herself and critical of other people. She can't stand the color her new neighbors painted their fence. Or the fact that the newspaper boy doesn't leave the paper right smack in front of her door. She thinks Aunt Andrea should buy less expensive clothes. And that my cousin, Devon, should get braces for his teeth. She tells me how to handle my emotions. She tries to psychoanalyze me. She tells me she knows how I'm feeling when she's so far off it's like a pathetic joke.

But despite all this, I know she's not mean. It's just that, for her, these things would make the world right. The only problem is, there's no end to them.

Mom explained it to me like this. "Your Nana is a good person," she said. "Perhaps she takes life a little too seriously, but deep down, she just wants us all to be happy. She wants us to be our best."

Mom was able to listen patiently to Nana. Nod sympathetically at her complaints. And for that reason, Nana Jean loved my mom. Dad could not have done better in choosing a wife.

Because of this, I know Jennifer doesn't stand much of a chance tonight. It won't be anything she does at Nana Jean's. Or anything she says. It's just that, well, I know Nana could never imagine Dad with anyone else. Not exactly shocking. It's hard for me to imagine Dad with anyone else. And I know for a long time, for Dad, it was hard to imagine Dad with anyone else.

Jenn looks wicked in the clothes I picked out for her. She comes to the house early, so I can do her hair. For the first half of the drive to Port Coquitlam, she asks questions about Nana. What are her interests? What was she like as a mom? Does she like chocolate? Does she like the kind of chocolates she bought her? And for the remaining part of the drive, she asks questions about herself. Do I look alright? What if she asks me to cook something? What if I inadvertently offend her? What if she doesn't like me at all?

I find it kind of funny. For a person in charge of an entire bank, meeting Nana has Jenn majorly unhinged.

"Relax!" Dad and I both tell her.

"She'll like you," says Dad. "And if she doesn't, well, that's her problem."

Jenn gives Dad this look. I know he's joking, but Jenn doesn't know him so well. He smiles at her. "I'm kidding. Of course, she'll like you. How could she not?"

Nana meets us at the front door. She gives me this stiff hug. But not before she tells me my hair is too long, my skirt is too short and I shouldn't wear such provocative nail polish.

Provocative? I look at my nails. I thought it was a cool shade of orange.

"Mom, I'd like you to meet Jennifer Reid," says Dad.

One thing about Nana is, she has this way of making

you real uncomfortable, just by being silent. She does this to Jenn right then. She stands back a little, looks at Jenn, folds her arms. "So, this is Jennifer," is all she says.

"Nice to meet you, Mrs. Collins." Jenn holds out her hand.

Nana takes it as Dad pushes past her into the house. "What's the problem with the garage door?" he asks.

We follow him in. Dad asks the question because he helps Nana with little things that go wrong around the house. Anything she can't fix. He doesn't mind. Grandpa was very good at woodwork and taught Dad how to work with tools. Dad tells lots of stories about the things they built in the shop.

"The pull has come loose and the screw broke when I tried to get it out."

"I'll take a look at it after we eat."

Nana has made all my favorites for dinner. Simple stuff that probably wouldn't bowl you over. But because Dad's cooking skills are limited to a frying pan and the barbecue, I never get them at home. Like roast chicken with stuffing and gravy. And apple crisp with a blob of whipped cream on the top.

Nana asks me her usual questions, between the "getting to know you" conversation with Jenn. You know the questions.

The "How's school?" question always comes first. Which, of course, I answer with, "Fine." Then comes

"What have you been up to lately?" to which I say, "Not much." Then there is some meaningless comment, and following that, since Nana happens to know about it, a question about how I did on some test. "You must be into final exams soon. How did you do on that math test?"

"Fine," I repeat.

At this point Dad always feels the need to speak up. This time he says, "Pam got a terrific mark on an English essay. Ninety-six percent."

Ahh. Now Nana has something to talk about. "Oh my, how clever! She's always done well in school," she tells Jenn. "She gets it from her mom."

"What about me?" demands Dad.

"Oh, and you too, dear, of course." She turns back to me. "Tell us, Pam, what do you want to be when you grow up?"

Aak! There it is again. Well, okay, Nana, since you asked. I'm going to be a shiftless drifter when I grow up. With no fixed address. If I said it, wouldn't that just blow her right out of her chair? But instead I say, "Don't know yet. I'm undecided. Maybe a writer of some type. Or — an artist." Then I get this brain attack. "Or maybe a banker like Jenn." I smile smugly. I'm not sure why I say it or why I smile like that. It's just one of those things you come out with. You know, just to shake things up.

"Oh," Jenn giggles, looking a little surprised. But

Dad gives me his sternest "watch it" look. Nana Jean does not like my answer at all.

"I see," she says, before doing that silent thing for a bit. "Like Jennifer."

After dinner Jenn and I help clear the table. Dad goes out to the garage. That's when things really start to fall apart. Jenn excuses herself to go to the washroom. While she is out of the room, Nana wants me to sit down at the kitchen table with her. She takes my hand in hers.

"She seems like a nice lady."

"Jenn? Oh, yeah. She says the odd weird thing once in a while, but inside, I think she's alright."

Nana listens. Then she looks at me in this curious way. "Of course," she begins, "whatever happens, you must never forget your mother."

Forget her? Forget my mother? Well, this is a tad inappropriate and out of the blue. I've been feeling alright up until now. Why would Nana say such a thing? Why would she want to wreck my evening just like that? And before I know it, the tears begin to squeeze right out.

Nana kind of panics. "Oh, now, Pam." She tugs a Kleenex from the box on the window sill. "Look what I've gone and done." She pats my eyes. "All I meant, dear, is, well, that comment you made about being a banker ..."

What is it with adults that they take everything you

say so literally? Can't we be allowed just one little joke? Anyway, I'm not listening. What makes her think I could ever, possibly, forget my mom? Doesn't she know how my whole world is ruined? The tears keep on flowing. My nose is running. Nana Jean searches for another box of Kleenex.

"I shouldn't have said anything," she fusses. "There now, Pammy," she pushes a wad of Kleenex into my face, "blow, dear. Come on. Blow hard."

I take the Kleenex and blow my nose. Hard. I'm having a full-blown breakdown again. I don't know what it is. It's been a whole year and I just can't get past hearing a reference to my mom without all the emotions jumbled inside gushing right out. I'm sniveling and honking. And I'm in this messy state when Jenn comes walking back in the room.

"Oh," I think I hear her say. She kind of hesitates, like she doesn't know whether she should stay or go.

Nana Jean has her arm around me. "Oh, Jennifer. Please, sit. It's all my fault. Poor Pammy. I just mentioned her mother. I should know better than that."

Yes, you should, I want to scream. I've told you before, I can handle my feelings myself. So just — just butt out.

"I'm always butting in where it's not my business." With her free hand, Nana tugs a Kleenex for herself. "I only want the best for my family," she sniffles. "Oh," she moans, a weak little cry like I've never heard before, "I love my family. I really do. I don't have anyone else. Not since Richard passed away." She takes her arm away from me and blows her own nose. Hard.

I'm surprised to see tears run down the wrinkles in Nana Jean's face. The face that only ever shows one emotion — none. Now I'm crying for her, as well as myself.

Jennifer looks all concerned. "Richard? That was your husband?" She takes Nana Jean's hand in her own.

Nana Jean is so sad, she can only nod.

"He must have been a wonderful man for you to miss him so much."

"Oh, he was," Nana kind of wails. "So full of life. He was always joking. He really made me laugh."

Jenn pats her hand. "Tell me something about him. I'd like to know Ken's dad."

Bingo! I don't know if Jenn planned it, but she sure hit on the right question. It sets Nana Jean on a roll. She talks for half an hour straight about Grandpa. About how they met. About how they furnished their apartment with cardboard boxes when they were first married, while she worked as a secretary and Grandpa took engineering at school. About the places they lived: Saudi Arabia, Germany, Japan, as his job took him around the world. About Dad and Uncle Sean being born, then later, Aunt Andrea and Uncle Nick. About their happy times and sick times, the good times and the bad. About how Grandpa found something good in every situation. And oh, how he loved his kids.

"Would you like to see a picture of Richard holding Ken just after he was born?"

"Yes, of course I would."

Nana opens the silver locket she wears around her neck. It holds a picture of Grandpa, looking very much like Dad does now, cuddling Dad as a baby on his lap. Grandpa has, like, this magnificent smile on his face.

"Oh," Jenn coos, holding it closer so she can get a better look. "This is so sweet." I don't know if it's too much dust in the air, or too much emotion, but Jenn dabs at her eye.

"Isn't it?" Nana dabs at her own eye again. "I have a whole album of them together if you'd like to see it."

"Oh, yes, I sure would."

Jennifer sniffs a little until Nana returns. Together they look at the album. The one I've seen many times before. Pictures of Grandpa and Dad together, fishing and working in the shop. Pictures of Dad as he was growing up. The album is titled, "Richard's Little Gaffer."

Nana sees Jenn looking at the title. "With the first one," she explains, "you get a little silly. They usually get the biggest fuss."

Jenn is obviously touched by it. She is majorly touched by it. Personally, I think it's the word gaffer that gets her all choked up. It's one of those words she would relate to. I mean, more than anyone else.

"Little gaffer," she splutters. "Isn't that just sooo sweet?"

I pass her the box of Kleenex. She passes it to Nana Jean. Nana passes it back to me. And although each one of us is doing it for our own reasons, we continue to snurf and snivel together. This is the state we are in when Dad returns from the garage. At first, he doesn't say anything. He just gets this horrified look.

"What on earth is going on in here?!"

"It's alright, dear," Nana begins to explain. "We were just having a little chat." Sniff. Sniff. Dad looks past her, at Jennifer with her eyes all red.

"A chat!" He looks at me. "Pamela, would you like to tell me what's going on in here?"

I would, Dad. But it's one of these women-knowing-women things that you really wouldn't get. "Like Nana said. We've been having a little chat."

He is not happy with my answer. He expected me to tell him more. He looks back at Jenn. "Are you alright?"

"Oh, yes." She blows her nose in this resounding sort of way. "Perfectly fine. Your mother is a wonderful lady. You're very lucky, Ken."

Seriously baffled, Dad rolls his eyes and shakes his head. He goes over to the sink to wash the grease off his hands.

We drive home in total silence. I know Dad is thinking the entire evening was a mega-bust. But I know better. I know Jenn got through to Nana Jean in a special kind of way. She let her talk about the person she loved. She let her remember him out loud. She listened while Nana told her how special Grandpa was. And how happy they'd been together. Jenn made Nana Jean smile.

THIRTEEN

June 2nd

Mr. Overhand, our social studies teacher, is really peeved. There is a stink bomb smoldering in the garbage can and he's demanding to know who's responsible. He's standing at the front of the classroom with his arms folded. His face is all shiny red and he's scanning us with these snarly black eyes.

"It's immature! That's what it is. This kind of trick," he stabs his finger toward the garbage can, "it's elementary school stuff! Now I want to know which one of you pin-headed adolescents refuses to grow up!" His eyes pass menacingly over each one of us.

No one moves. No one says a thing. Not surprising. Who would admit to being the pin-headed adolescent who refuses to grow up? Especially to an overexcited social studies teacher who's ready to rip someone apart?

"I see," Mr. Overhand says, slowly nodding his head. "I see. Alright, if that's the way it's going to be, you are ALL going to sit here until one of you cracks. And I don't care if that takes all night!"

Mr. Overhand returns to his desk. He sits down and pours another cup of coffee from his mega-thermos. He takes a book out of his drawer and leans back in his chair, like he's prepared to do just that. Camp here, in this foul-smelling room, all night, until one of us pin-heads cracks.

This brings major groans from all of us. It's ten after three and the thought of dragging this school day out one minute longer than necessary really kind of sucks. Darla Miller is getting her hair permed at four o'clock. Joanne is going to a movie with Tony. John has a guitar lesson. Mike Ortega is supposed to help his dad in his shop. Danielle is meeting Matt Leighton at 3:30.

"I don't usually show up until at *least* half an hour after I'm supposed to. It's good to keep a guy hanging on. But I do need the time to freshen my makeup."

Oh, right. No doubt for him fresh makeup is worth the half an hour you make him hang around waiting.

Linda has a drama practice. And me? Well, I don't really have much to do. I told Dad I'd clean the bathrooms after school. But I can sit here and wait. In fact, I think I'd rather.

Mr. O doesn't want to hear any of our excuses anyway.

Know something? I know who did it. It was Justin Randall. I saw him stuffing matches into a blue pen at lunchtime. I passed him in the cafeteria. He was sitting in a corner by himself and that's what he was doing. He was keeping it low, between his legs. It was the goofy expression on his face that made me look to see what he was doing. When he saw me looking, he turned his back. But he continued to assemble the stink bomb. I don't think anyone else saw him. I've been wondering this afternoon when he was going to set if off.

Mr. O is right about one thing. Justin Randall has never grown up. I think his brain sort of cut out somewhere around fourth grade. I often wonder what he's doing in grade nine. Nothing seems to make any sense to him. And he stopped asking questions three years ago. Which, in a sad sort of way, was good. His questions were usually really stupid and took up a ton of class time. But he still shows up, I guess because he has to. He doesn't do anything. He just sits there at the back of the room and amuses himself. He mostly draws. Pictures of sports cars and hot rods with sparks and lightning bolts flying out. Actually, they're really quite good. And colorful. If you happen to like that kind of stuff. Once in a while, he hands something in. With no content to speak of, but with some intricately drawn, far-out title page. And at the end of the year, he's moved up a grade.

I feel him looking at me. I glanced at him just a few seconds ago. He gave me this dark, supposed-to-be-terrifying, Freddy Krueger warning look. He's way too slow to be subtle. To maintain a poker face. So I won't look at him anymore. Don't worry your short-circuited brain there, Justin. If you don't give yourself away, I won't. I'm in no rush to clean the bathrooms.

The final bell goes. Out of habit, we all stand up. Mr. O only has to look over his glasses to make us sit down again. We fold our binders and stuff them into our backpacks. May as well be ready to leave when the culprit confesses. If he does. We watch out the window as the mature adolescents spill onto the school grounds. Laughing, yelling, gobbing on the sidewalks, punching each other, hanging from the trees. After about fifteen minutes Mr. O looks up from his book again. "Well? Is anyone ready to fess up?"

Nope. No one is ready to fess up. But Mr. O, if my dad wasn't dating her, you'd get along just fine with Jennifer Reid.

Joanne and I are writing notes back and forth. What's with Shauna Whittaker's bra showing? Couldn't she find a shirt big enough to cover it up?

I look at Shauna's backless halter top. Hmm. I write back: Well, if she's going to have her bra show, she should at least tuck in the label, instead of advertising her size.

Linda and Darla are also writing notes. Mandeep is asking Danny about our math homework. John is rolling paper into balls and hurling them at the garbage can. Two rims and one swish! Carl Jenkins is eating a bag of nachos. The cheesy smell combined with the stink bomb is enough to make me sick. Danielle is filing her fingernails. And Justin Randall is working with his head down. He's intent on his sketching. I think he's already forgotten it's because of him we're all still here. Another fifteen minutes passes. Danielle has finished her nails. She takes out a compact and checks her makeup in the mirror. She adds a little more color and snaps it shut. She looks at her watch.

"I have to go," she says, standing up.

"Sit down, young lady," is Mr. O's answer. "No one leaves until someone takes responsibility for that stink bomb."

"Well, it's not like I did it. Mr. O, I think you and I both know that!"

"Sit down."

"This sucks." Danielle grudgingly sits down at her desk. "This is stupid." She looks at her watch. "Why should I have to sit here? I didn't do it. Look." Danielle peers around the room. She bounces to her feet again. "Whoever did it, just say so. Okay? I have to go."

The request is so self-centered, some of us start to laugh.

"It's not funny." Her eyes narrow on Mike Ortega who is laughing the loudest. "Mike, was it you?"

"No." Mike's laugh dissolves into a frown. "It wasn't me."

"Danny?"

Danny looks up from his homework. "Go away."

"John? John Robbel? I could see it. I bet it was you."

John flings another ball of paper. "It wasn't me, Higgins. Why don't you just sit down."

Mr. O still holds his book as if he's reading. But his glasses are lowered as he watches us from behind his desk.

Danielle continues to scan the room for a likely suspect. She spies Carl Jenkins munching nachos in the corner. She faces Mr. Overhand. "Alright. I'll tell you who did it. But only if you make sure he stays away from me."

Mr. O doesn't agree, but taps the infamous pen, which was the stink bomb, on his desk.

"Carl Jenkins did it."

"Huh?" Carl's hand freezes on the way to his mouth. He hears his name spoken, but at that moment isn't quite sure what he's done.

Mr. O stands up. "Is that true, Jenkins? You set the stink bomb?"

"What?" Carl stops chewing. He struggles to sit up in his desk. "What are you talking about?"

"You did so!" insists Danielle. "I saw him making it. He set it off while you were passing out the worksheets."

Carl finally clues in. "I did not! Higgins, you're full of it. Don't listen to her. She's making it up."

Mr. Overhand frowns as he looks from one to the other.

"Oh, yeah? Well, I can prove it. Mr. O, look closely at that pen in your hand. My guess is it's an aqua-blue Paper-Mate."

Mr. O looks at the pen. It *is* an aqua-blue Paper-Mate. But then, so is mine. And so is Danielle's. We'd all been given them by Mr. Bartell. He'd set out a box during our last exam.

"She's right, Jenkins. This bomb was made from a Paper-Mate. Alright, all of you can go. Except you, Jenkins. You stay right where you are."

Danielle is the first one out the door.

"And don't forget your homework, the ten review questions at the end of chapter fourteen."

"But she's lying! She's making the whole thing up! Look, Danny's got a Paper-Mate! Linda's got a Paper-Mate!"

Save your breath, Carl. Reasoning at this point is useless. By now, half the class has left the room. No one is going to listen to you. Mr. O has his culprit. And we have our freedom.

"Carl Jenkins, you and I are going down to visit Mrs. Lofts."

Why didn't I tell Mr. O what I knew? I watched Justin Randall look up and notice for the first time that everyone was gone. He placed the winged hot rod he was drawing in a notebook. He slowly packed his books away and wandered out the door. Maybe I should have. But I knew Carl Jenkins had enough going for him that he could take it. He was sharp. He'd get out of it. Justin Randall wouldn't have a chance. If what he did had hurt someone, then definitely, I would have said something. But a stink bomb? It was the work of a childish mind trying to have some fun.

FOURTEEN

June 7th

Do you ever get so sick of everything in your life, you just want to quit? Like when you look in the mirror in the morning and you see the same dull face stare back. Or you go into the kitchen and you hear your dad's same old voice. Or you walk down the hall at school with your so-called-friends, talking about the same old stuff. Or you go from boring class to even more boring class, predicting with one-hundred-percent accuracy what's going to happen next. Like, Mr. Bartell is going to tell Rudy Lantz to put his penknife away. Rudy's going to ignore him. Mr. Bartell's going to say it again.

Rudy's going to say, "Make me," and Mr. Bartell is going to march him down to see Mrs. Lofts. And you're thinking, like, so, this is it? My big excitement for the day is watching Rudy Lantz butt heads with Mr. Bartell? Maybe you don't get like that. It's probably just me.

That's how I've been feeling this week. I'm lying on my bed with my headphones on. I'm listening to The Wallflowers. Not even the jars of nature on my bookshelf can cheer me up. I look at them, sitting there, classified by material. You know, like earth, water, minerals and stuff. Then alphabetical by place. I just realized something. I don't have a jar of Ninety Foot. I never thought to get one. Maybe that's what I'm missing in my life.

I don't have any friends again. Ever since Joanne and Tony Lasserman stumbled onto each other in the Canyon. They've been hanging around together every night. Getting to know one another after all this time. So near, and yet so far. "He picks his little sister up from day care after school. He helps her on with her coat. Pam, he's just, like, this really sensitive guy!"

It's enough to make me gag.

Mandeep and Danny have this thing going on. Ever since I had them for dinner. They just really hit it off. And Linda's hanging out with Darla Miller. She's decided she likes Darla's brother. That one's a littler harder to get. He wears combats. Not sometimes. But all the time. Like they really mean something. And this spiked dog collar around his neck.

Everybody's noticing everybody. Except me. It's like this major thing to get involved before Mike Ortega's year-end party. So you don't show up alone. Good thing I don't have to worry about it. Seeing as how Joanne got me involved for me. I know I don't have. to go along with it. But I don't care enough to care.

Besides, I have an excuse. I'm weird.

"How can you not be excited?" my former friends ask me. "We're graduating from junior high!"

"Yeah? So? It's hardly like the biggest event of my life."

They just shake their heads. "Pam, sometimes you act so weird."

Joanne's been wearing so much black around her eyes lately, she looks like some kind of ghoul from *Night of the Living Dead*. Linda dyed her hair lime green and is wearing it spiked. She had her ears pierced right to the top. She pierced her nose, one eyebrow and, since hanging out with Darla's brother, her belly-button too. For all I know, there could be other places. And I'm weird.

Maybe it's true. But I just can't get excited about anything. It doesn't appeal to me to put goop all over my face. I can't shriek with excitement when someone does something different with their hair. I like my life calm. I like it arranged. If I get through the day without anything abnormal happening, it's good. I'm getting by being boring. It works. To survive, I guess I don't need anything else. Still, I'm getting real tired of my same dull face.

When I was ten, my grandma, Mom's mom, died of multiple sclerosis. She had it all my life. She lived in the extended-care unit of the hospital. I used to visit her with Mom. We went at the same time every Saturday after lunch. We brought her the same kind of cookies and the same kind of novels so she would have something to read that week. Grandma was always sitting in her wheelchair at the same table in the cafeteria. She could only move her head. In front of her was one of the books, propped open on a music stand. Paper clips were attached to the pages. When Grandma finished a page, she bent forward and, catching the paper clip, turned it with her nose. She spoke very slowly, taking lots of breaks. And when she finished, she was always out of breath. I could not understand her, but Mom could.

I would look around the room and see the same people doing the same thing. Mr. Cruikshank was always shaking the tray on his wheelchair. Trying to break out. He'd been in a car accident and was missing a piece of his brain. Mrs. Grewal was always dancing by herself in a corner. To music only she could hear. A man in his twenties lay on a bed with his eyes closed, soaking up the sun. He was surrounded by pictures his three-year-old daughter had drawn for him. Mr. Jones, a very, very old man, a pilot in the war, sat in a corner and smoked a pipe. He blew smoke rings in the air. And a girl my age, with big scared eyes, lay very still in a large crib, watching something, I don't know what, maybe just the shadows dancing across the walls.

At one o'clock the physical therapist would come in. She would have them do exercises. Lift a finger, nod their head, make a circle with their foot, whatever they were able to do. At one-thirty she would leave.

"Mom," I said one day as we left the hospital. "Those people are always doing the same thing. It's like they're waiting for something to happen. Just sitting there, passing time. They need some excitement in their lives."

"No, Pam. It only seems that way to you and me. They are content. They need the routine. It may be hard for you to understand, but they do well when their days are arranged. They know what to expect. Some of them have lived through more excitement than anyone needs in their lives."

And they continued like that. Every time we went, it was the same old thing. I got so bored, sometimes Mom would send me down to the gift shop to buy a comic or a magazine. Then at Christmas, Santa Claus came. He ho, ho, ho'd around the cafeteria, passing out presents, bellowing out Merry Christmas in his big booming voice. There were many relatives and little children running all around. The Boy Scouts put on a skit and a choir from the nearby United Church sang carols, inviting the relatives to all join in. There was food and punch and lots of noise. Too much noise for Mr. Cruikshank, who began to scream and bang on his tray. Too much for Mrs. Grewal, who rolled herself in a ball and cringed against the floor. Mr. Jones gave up smoking and returned to his room. And the girl my age, with her big scared eyes, opened her mouth and made an almost-silent terrified noise.

When we returned two weeks later, peace had been restored. Mrs. Grewal danced with a smile on her face. Mr. Jones smoked happily. My grandma read her book, with three others stacked in a pile beside her. At one o'clock, the physical therapist came in. They did their exercises without any complaints. They followed their routine. They all seemed content. They were sick and old.

I'm not. And I sure am getting tired of Rudy Lantz, Mr. Bartell and my same dull face.

FIFTEEN

June 9th

Dad and Jenn took me out to buy a puppy last night. She's sleeping on my lap as I write. She is so adorable you just can't believe it. She's a basset hound, she's twelve weeks old and her name is — guess what? — Emily. Jenn helped me with that. Her ears are so long, she trips over them when she walks. She takes a step, trips on her ear, does a somersault and starts again. I'm allowed to keep her kennel in my room, as long as she sleeps in it during the night. I couldn't make her last night. She looked way too neglected with her sad eyes and nose sticking out between the bars. I let her curl up next to me on the bed. I mean, seeing as it was her first night away from her mother. As if I don't know what that feels like that.

It was quite a surprise. I was just coming in from a walk in the canyon. Dad and Jenn were sitting at the kitchen table. They had these looks on their faces like they knew something I didn't know. Not something bad, but like something they wanted to tell me, but they were going to have some fun with it first. By playing it real cool. You know the kind of humor, kind of feeble.

"So, what's up?" asked Dad when I came in the door.

"Nothin'," I said. I dropped my backpack on the floor next to the refrigerator. I looked at Dad. Then over at Jenn. They both had these big smiley eyes. "What *is* up?"

"How was your walk in the park?"

Dad won't call it the canyon. He won't even hint that it's anything other than this green playing field, where, unless you're playing some contact sport, you could not possibly get hurt. He hates me going down there. He tried to forbid me at first. We had this big argument when it finally came out that he was afraid I might do what Mom did. We both ended up crying when I told him I had a little more common sense than that.

"It was alright. Mrs. Marshall's still looking for Krissy." I poured myself a glass of juice. "She's got hip waders on and she's stumbling down the creek, trying to peer through the water. But she's not looking for

Krissy's body. Just Krissy's pink sweater. She's absolutely convinced Krissy's still alive."

As I answered his question, the smile in Dad's eyes faded. "How do you know what she's thinking?"

I shrugged. "I asked her. The thing is, her eyes are so bloodshot, everything she sees must be through a haze of pink. Everything must look like Krissy's sweater." I finished my juice. "So, what's up?"

Dad took a minute to tear himself from what I had said. He reconfigured his smile. "As you know, Pam, I'm not too crazy about you walking in the park all alone."

I rolled my eyes. "Dad, haven't we been through all that? I'm not going to do anything stu – "

Dad interrupted me by holding his hand up for silence. "So, we're going to get you a companion."

"Oh, yeah? What kind of companion? Some bald Mr. Clean to walk five steps behind me with his thick arms crossed wherever I go? Some ... some – " See, I was kind of ticked off because Dad says these things sometimes that really mean, in his not-so-subtle way, that he doesn't trust me. And I wish he'd quit it, because it's really insulting. Well, and okay, maybe just once in a while it's my fault. Maybe once or twice I've jumped to conclusions. But if it weren't for his attitude, I wouldn't get so stressed out.

Jenn wasn't sure if she should giggle or not. Mainly because she doesn't know about Dad and his attitude yet, and why I was all hyped up.

Dad just glared at me, waiting for my seizure to blow over. "No, I was thinking more like a dog."

It took me only a second to forgive him. "Really? A dog?"

"Really," said Dad. His smile returned. "Jenn knows a good breeder in Richmond. What do you think?"

I had wanted a dog for a long time, and Dad knew it. I had asked for one many times. I'd asked for a kitten, a hampster. I'd even said, "Well, okay then, how about a white rat?"

To which Dad had made this face like he had worms in his mouth. "A rat?!"

"Some people think they're good pets."

"Yeah, weird people," said Dad.

It wasn't that Dad didn't like animals. The problem was Dad's old collie, B.B., who died when I was three. Dad had had him since he was a teenager. He told me he was the smartest dog there ever was. He had a sixth sense. All Dad had to do was think of something he needed and B.B. would show up with whatever it was. Like the time Dad was standing on a ladder, fixing the siding on our house. A story I've heard about a hundred zillion times in my life. Dad realized he'd left the hammer in the basement. He started to climb down. Sitting on the ground at the base of the ladder was B.B., with the hammer in his mouth. Dad knew he couldn't replace B.B. So he wouldn't even try.

"When can we go?"

"How about right now?"

And that's how I acquired Emily. I could tell right away she was the creative one of the litter. She figured out how to squeak the toy football I gave her faster than any of the other pups. And she was curious, but not pushy, just cautious. I gave all the puppies a treat. Emily sniffed hers, but she watched her brothers and sisters eat before eating it herself. I picked her up. When she licked my cheek, I just knew she was the right one. Then Dad took her, and she licked his cheek. "Yup," he said.

Everyone's a sucker for a pup.

Wait until I tell you about taking her for a walk in the canyon after school today. Actually, it was more of a carry. I just wanted to show her around. I carried her to where the wooden bridge crosses the creek. I stayed away from Ninety Foot. I thought the roar of the water might scare her to death. Like I said before, it can be pretty terrifying for someone who's not used to it. Even if you *are* used to it, for the first few minutes it always reminds you of how puny you really are.

We'd walked down to the creek and were on our way back up again. I was carrying her up the ten billion steps from the bottom of the gorge to the world above. She can't handle steps yet. Up or down.

Anyway, guess who's leaning against the railing at the top, talking to a couple of friends? I'll give you a hint. I was all hot and sweaty and out of breath, my hair looked like it had been styled by a lightning strike and I was wearing total grunge clothes in case Emily peed on me. It was Matt Leighton, of course. Leaning there, all calm and cool, with shoulders gorgeously stooped. And one very wicked smile.

I couldn't exactly turn around. So I continued to huff and puff up the steps, like some kind of squinty mollusk finding its way out of the dark. I thought it best to keep my head down and talk to Emily. He might not notice me slither right by. It didn't work. I was almost at the top when I saw him make a sign to his friends and move away from them. He was waiting on the top step.

"Those are killer steps," he said. "Here, let me take your puppy while you catch your breath."

I was so shocked to hear him speak to me, I didn't mean to, but I clutched Emily tighter to my chest.

"It's okay. I like dogs." He smiled as I let him have Emily.

His grin took what little breath I had left completely away. Say something. Quick, Pam, you doorknob. I dug out this memory of him playing with Mr. Spinelli's German shepherd, Lupus.

"I know what you like," I wheezed in this hoarse voice like some kind of telephone pervert. "I mean, I know you like dogs."

"Oh yeah? How do you know?" Interested, he pet Emily.

"I saw you." I felt so stupid. He probably thought

I'd been following him around. "I mean, I passed you on the street and saw you playing with Mr. Spinelli's dog." My breath had returned. Matt seemed quite satisfied with my answer.

"Ahh, yeah, well, you'd have to be heartless not to give him a little attention. He's such a nice dog." He gave Emily a squeeze.

Oh, to be Emily in your arms, Matt Leighton. To be held against that amazing bod.

"What's his name?"

"Lupus."

"Hey, Lupus," he stroked Emily's chin, "you've got the same name as Spinelli's dog."

"Oh, no — he's Emily. I mean, he's a she. She's Emily. I thought you were still talking about Lupus. You know, Mr. Spinelli's dog. Because, I mean, since we'd been talking about him, just like — " Oh, this is good. Keep blundering on, Pam. I'm sure he's really impressed by now.

Matt was laughing. He spoke to Emily. "Tell her not to sweat it, Emily. Know what? I like your name. It's musical." He looked at me. "What's yours?"

"Mine?" I punched my finger to my chest.

Matt studied my face. He studied the woods behind me. He looked over one, then the other shoulder. He glanced to his left, and then to his right. Clearly, as any numskull could see, there was no one else around. Grinning, he looked back at me. "Yeah, yours."

"Pamela. Pamela Collins."

"My name's Matt Leighton."

Like, no duh. As if I didn't know. "Hi, Matt."

"Listen, Pamela. Can I walk with you? Are you on your way somewhere?"

All I could think of was why he'd have the least bit of interest in walking with me, when he had the likes of Danielle Higgins. It had to be Emily. I mean, like I said, everybody's a sucker for a puppy. "Sure, if you want to. I'm on my way home."

The end of this completely unbelievable story is that Matt Leighton walked all the way down Ross Road with me, down Hoskins and down my street to my house. Sometimes he carried Emily. Sometimes I did. And for a little stretch, she waddled between us. Standing outside my house, he talked about his dog, Swat. He talked about his job at the Westview Safeway. He told me he'd seen me many times in the canyon. Lying on the white rock down by Ninety Foot. Soaking up the sun. Looking very content with my life. He told me he goes there a lot himself. You know, just to figure things out. And he never once mentioned Danielle Higgins. Then he said, "Well, see you." And I said, "Yeah, see you."

And that was that. And I discovered that I really like him. I mean, aside from his wicked grin and perfect body. Although, I'm sitting here with Emily on my lap, trying to figure out what that entire thing was all about.

SIXTEEN

June 10th

Joanne's grounded Saturday night and can't go to Mike Ortega's party. This means I won't be able to go with John Robbel. Oh, poor me, I'm in such distress.

She called Mr. Bartell a slippery old coot, and it got back to her mom. I was there in gym class when it happened. We were doing the swing in social dance. And this time Joanne got Mr. Bartell for her partner.

It was pretty funny to watch. Mr. Bartell ripped her around the gym much faster than when I danced with him. He huffed and puffed and yelled out instructions — that is, when he could catch his breath to talk.

He taught us half-rotations, wraps and unwraps, rows and the double-cross. He demonstrated single-unders and double-unders. And all the time he had this real happy look on his face. In fact, he was so into it, I wondered why he didn't teach at a dance studio. Instead of boring old English to us.

Joanne had this totally serious expression. Sort of, like, this "Get me out of here or I might throw up" look on her face. I had to giggle with everyone else. Although I did feel just a twinge of sympathy. Having been there myself. I mean, the sweat and the breath and everything.

So, what happened was, Mr. Bartell did one of those double-under things and suddenly swung Joanne away from him. Joanne's hand slipped from his, she lost her balance and fell on her butt. Mr. Bartell helped her get back up again. He apologized all over the place. He felt real bad about it, I could tell. He said it was his fault. She wasn't expecting it and he should have warned her. But from experience, I suspected differently. Because of the major sweat factor involved, it was hard to hang onto his hand. Whatever. He told us to get into partners and he let Joanne go.

I know Joanne was real embarrassed, and that's what made her as mad she was. She was angry with herself more than Mr. Bartell. Still, as she walked back toward us, she muttered, "It wouldn't have happened if he wasn't such a slippery old coot."

She didn't know that Mr. Bartell was directly behind her. Which would have been alright, because he didn't hear her. The problem was, Danielle did. And because Danielle had never got over the fact that Steve Adler had gone for Joanne and not her, she would never miss a chance to humiliate her. Not one chance in her entire life.

Facing Joanne, watching Mr. Bartell come up behind her, Danielle stepped forward. "What did you say, Joanne?"

"I said — I fell because he's a slippery old coot!"

Everybody around her went quiet. Including Mr. Bartell. It was one of those situations you wish you could rewind and live through over again. After considering if it was worth hurting whoever got hurt.

"Joanne?" Mr. Bartell said after a few silent moments. His scraggy beard was tilted in the air. And his thin lips were set tight.

Joanne's eyes grew huge as she realized he had heard what she said. She was silent as she turned around.

"I just wanted to make sure you're alright?"

She nodded quietly. "Uh-huh. Yes, I'm alright. Thank you."

Mr. Bartell clapped his hands. "Alright, class. Let's hop to it. Come on. Come on! It's time to swing, everyone." But he didn't seem nearly as enthusiastic as he was before.

Joanne turned back toward us. Her eyes bore into

125

Danielle, declaring total, killer war.

Mr. Bartell didn't phone Mrs. Robertson or anything like that. What happened was, Linda went over
to Joanne's house after school. Joanne told me all this,
in really major detail, about two hours ago on the phone.
They were sitting in the family room looking through
old issues of YM. Out of the blue, Linda just started to
giggle. Not about anything, as far as Joanne could tell.
Mrs. Robertson was getting supper ready in the kitchen.
It's separated from the family room by a low rail.

"What's so funny?" Joanne asked her.

Linda kept on giggling. "I was just thinking of the
look on Bartell's face when you called him a slippery
old coot."

Joanne's mom looked up from chopping a green
pepper (Joanne even told me what she was chopping).
She saw her mom looking, and listening, and the way
her eyes got narrow. Joanne made crazy signals for Linda
to be quiet.

"Old coot. No kidding, I thought those old eyeballs would pop right out!"

"Joanne?" Mrs. Robertson said. I knew exactly the
tone she used. Like the time we spray-painted the front
door orange, was how Joanne described it.

Joanne jumped up. "Mom, don't worry about it.
He never heard me."

Joanne's mom placed one hand on a hip.

Linda was, like, totally oblivious to Mrs. Robertson.

"What are you talking about?" She kept on laughing. "Of course, he heard you!"

When Joanne's mom heard that, she got this real hostile look.

By now Joanne was fuming. "Linda. Will you shut up!"

"Joanne Robertson! I am ashamed of you! How could you say such a thing to your teacher?" Mrs. Robertson waved her chopping knife in the air.

"Oops," said Linda.

"Thanks!" said Joanne.

"Well — gee." Linda glanced at her watch. "It's getting real late. I guess I'd better go."

"I hope you apologized," said Mrs. Robertson, after Linda had left. "You did apologize, didn't you?"

"Well — sort of."

"You didn't, did you?"

"Well — not in so many words."

Mrs. Robertson pulled the telephone book from out of a drawer. "Well, in so many words — you're going to do it right now." She brought it to Joanne in the family room and dropped it in her lap. "Look him up."

"Mom! I can't call Mr. Bartell! It's ... it's ... it can only be a negative experience!"

"You listen to me, young lady. I'll have many more negative experiences in store for you if you don't phone and apologize to your teacher right now! Honestly, I am embarrassed. How do you think this reflects on me and your dad?"

According to Joanne, that was the very moment Mr. Robertson picked to walk in the door. And, like Joanne and me agreed, dads usually aren't too swift at cluing in to these kinds of "situations."

"What reflects on me?" Mr. Robertson said cheerily, hanging up his jacket. "Her charming good looks?"

By this time, Mrs. Robertson was really riled. "The fact that your daughter called her teacher an old coot!"

"I didn't mean anything by it!"

"How was he supposed to know that?!"

It was then that Mr. Robertson got the idea that maybe something was just a tad wrong. He held up his hands. "Okay, wait a minute. What did you call him?"

Joanne didn't answer.

"An old coot," said her mom.

"Really?" Her dad bit his lips so as not to smirk.

"Paul! It's not funny! You're only encouraging her insolent behavior! Joanne, you're grounded for a week!"

"What? That's not fair! I didn't mean to say it! It just came out! I don't even know what 'coot' means! I got it from Dad!"

"Me?!"

With this totally ticked-off expression, Mrs. Robertson faced Mr. Robertson. She folded her arms. Joanne sounded real stern when she repeated what her mom said. "And just who were you calling an old coot?"

Mr. Robertson didn't answer.

"Who was your dad calling an old coot? Joanne?"

Her mom was so stressed, Joanne had no choice but to answer, "Grandma."

Joanne's dad gave her this demon look. Like she was some kind of a traitor or something.

"My mother? You called my mother an old coot?!"

"I don't believe this. How did I get dragged into this?"

"Answer me, Paul. Did you call my mother an old coot?"

Joanne's dad didn't answer. He just made this face at Joanne.

"Paul?!"

"Alright. Alright. I may have. Just once."

"Just once?"

"Yeah. The time she stood over my back when I was laying her tile floor. 'It's too far to the left. It's too far to the right. That piece is cracked. Shouldn't the corner come up a bit? It's not level! Do you even know what you're doing?' Man, it was all I could do not to tell the old coot to do it herself!"

"My mother is *not* an old coot! She's a perfection-ist, that's all!"

"She's an old coot! What are you going to do, Susie? Ground me too?!"

Mr. Robertson didn't get grounded, but from what Joanne said, their supper was real intense tonight.

She phoned me again five minutes ago. She's still grounded, except for Saturday night. She told her mom, get this, that I was really looking forward to Ortega's party because I had met some guy I really liked. She didn't want to disappoint me by not being able to go. Mrs. Robertson is a pushover when it comes to me, and Joanne knows it. She'd do somersaults off a spring-board if she thought it would make me laugh. She'd do anything to make me happy. Including letting Joanne break her curfew. So, I guess I'm going to be seeing John Robbel Saturday night.

SEVENTEEN

June 11th

I found something tonight that I didn't know was missing. But am I ever glad to get it back. This has happened to me a lot in the last few months. I mean, finding something, or maybe I should say discovering something, that I didn't know was gone. I'm not talking about a favorite shirt or anything like that. The things I keep discovering are intangible. I can't touch or see them or even put any kind of label on them. The real importance of them is how they make me feel. Like I said, this has been happening to me a lot in the last two months. And all of these things I've been finding disappeared with Mom.

I know this sounds really weird, but an example is, like, the comics in *The Vancouver Sun*. Before Mom, I read them every morning before school. I had read them ever since I can remember. It got so, like, if I didn't read them, because the paper was late or I was late or something, I felt like I had missed part of the morning. Not that they're so uproariously funny or anything. But because they made me smile a little. They made me feel kind of good. It was something I just did. Reading them gave me sort of a sense of completion. Like my morning routine was finished and it was time to move on to school.

Whatever, I couldn't read them after Mom died. I couldn't read anything after Mom. I'd read the first two comics or even the first page in a book, and realize I couldn't remember what I'd just read. I had no memory of it and absolutely no concentration to continue on. You can just imagine how hard this made school. Anyway, I can't even remember what I did with my mornings last fall. That's how bad my memory got. All I can remember is that every day was total chaos. It was routine enough. Just, like, completely confused.

It was on the Christmas holidays, seven months after Mom died, that I discovered the comics again. At first, I read only one or two. Short ones, like *Family Circus* and *Bizarro*. Then, after a few days, I got through *Fox Trot* and *Overboard*. By the end of the holidays, I was reading all of them again. And I've kept it up. It's just one of those things that's put a little order back into my life. Besides, they can be funny every once in a while. I just realized something. I even read a whole book this spring. Cover to cover. And I liked it too. I read *Lord of the Flies*.

What got me started on all this was hearing my dad laugh. When I say laugh in this case, I don't mean like a little chortle or guffaw or whatever you'd call it. I mean one of those big, thunderous, side-splitting outbursts that really means something. Like Grandpa used to have.

It happened when Emily and I were down in the basement watching TV. Dad and Jenn were in the living room above us. I don't know what they were doing or even talking about. That's beside the point. I just heard Jenn's voice and then Dad broke into this big happy laugh. The kind of laugh that comes from deep down inside of you. The kind that takes over the moment. The kind that is only possible when whatever you heard or saw was the focus of your attention. Consuming is what I'd call it. No kidding, it was a consuming laugh. And the thing of it is, you know it can only come from someone who is completely relaxed.

Right then, Dad's laugh was the focus of my attention. It had been a long, long time since I had heard it. It made me feel so good. It made me think of a lot of things. But mostly about how he used to be funny. And about how much fun we used to have. And I didn't realize until that moment how much I had missed that.

Now I'm wondering how many other things I'm missing that I don't even know about. And if I'll ever get them back.

EIGHTEEN

June 13th

Joanne phoned me at 7:00 this morning to find out what I'm going to wear tonight.

"Are you nuts, Jo? I don't plan on getting up for three hours. The last thing on my mind is what I'm going to wear to Ortega's party!"

"I thought I'd wear my black stretch lace top and my white jeans."

"Good. I'm glad for you. Now, can I go back to sleep?"

"On second thought ... " I could hear Joanne drumming her fingers against something. She was ignoring me. This was going to take a while. I clutched my knees and curled up on the bed. "No, on second thought, I'll wear my stretch top and black jeans. Yeah, black jeans."

I yawned. "Even better. You'll look exquisite. Totally awesome. Now I'm going back to sleep."

"And shoes — should I wear my chunky heels or strappy sandals?"

"Chunky heels." I thought it best to answer. If I didn't, she'd only drag this out by agonizing over it anyway. Besides, her chunky heels make her taller than me. "Good, you're dressed. Now, I'm going to hang up."

"Pam — what about my hair!"

"Joanne. At this minute I don't want to hear about your hair. We're going to a lousy party with the same people we see every day. Not exactly to dinner with Jakob Dylan. Mike's parents will be there. In fact, it was their big idea. We'll probably be forced to play Twister and eat Pringles. We won't even get to watch Carl Jenkins puke. Now, I want to go back to sleep!"

"Fine! Just fine for you, Pam. You haven't been stuck in the house after school all week!"

This made me feel a little sorry for her. Joanne is real social compared to me. She likes to be around people. She likes to talk and she likes action. She gets bored out of her skull when we go walking in Lynn Canyon Park. Still, we've always got along. Probably because when we're together, she gets to talk all the time, while all I have to do is pretend to listen. This works for both of us. When I'm quiet, it makes her think that what she has to say is important. While it leaves me to think of other stuff. Anyway, her mom sure picked the punishment to fit the person. For Joanne, being stuck in her room was truly traumatic. For me, well, for one thing, I don't think anyone would notice.

"Okay," I said. "What were you thinking for your hair?"

I tried to get out of the party right to the end. Dad was over at Nana Jean's fixing a leaky toilet. When he phoned to say he'd be longer than he'd planned, I thought I had it made. Someone had to stay home and care for Emily.

"That's okay, Dad. Not a problem. I'll stay home and watch Emily. You take as long as you want."

Dad was quiet as he thought about this. It must have been the calm in my voice that gave me away. "Oh no, you won't. You're going to that party."

I don't know what it is about him. But I'm sure that if he could arrange my life for me, he wouldn't leave a single day where I could just be by myself.

"I'll look after Emily."

He didn't say how he was going to do this *and* fix the leaky toilet, but five minutes later, the phone rang. It was Jenn. She'd be right over.

I wasn't wearing anything devastating or anything

like that. Just this sleeveless white shirt Jenn had a lady at one of her executive stores pick out for me. And a pair of khaki pants. But when I opened the door a while later, "Pam, you look stunning!" is what Jenn said. She didn't come in right away, but stood there, just looking at me, moving her head back and forth. Like she couldn't believe it. "Absolutely stunning."

She gave me this great big hug.

It was nice of her to compliment me. But I thought she was overstating it just a tad. Okay, I guess the tan I picked up in the canyon goes well with my white shirt. And maybe my hair being curled kind of works for me. Aside from that, I'd swept just a little blush high up on my cheeks. Oh, and I used the "nasty" red lipstick Joanne insisted I get because it looked "deadly" on me. But only a tiny touch. But me — stunning? I thought Danielle Higgins set the standard for that.

"What's wrong? Isn't that an okay word?"

"Yeah," I shrugged. "It's okay. I mean, there's nothing wrong with it. It's cool. It's just, I've never thought I could look anything like that."

Jenn gave me another big hug. "It's not only your looks, Pam. You're a beautiful young lady, both inside and out." With her arm around me, she steered us into the house.

I'm almost embarrassed to write this down. It's just that it made me feel kind of good. Kind of, for a moment, happy about myself. Not that I believe it or anything. But because Jenn sounded totally serious, I don't think she was trying to con me at all. If she was, she was pretty good at it.

"You may as well get used to it," she continued. "You're going to be turning heads for many years to come."

I started to get squirmy. I'm not used to being told I'm pretty good stuff. Except by my family, of course. But they're not going to tell me anything else. Jenn must have clued in that I was becoming seriously embarrassed. She changed the subject right away.

"Where's that Emily I'm supposed to be looking after?"

Emily came in from the kitchen, wagging her tail, loudly squeaking her plastic football.

Jenn called her over. "Good girl! That's dyno music you're playing, Em."

I kind of flinched. "Dyno?"

"Yeah." Jenn bent down to pet Emily. "You know, like dynamite. Dynamite music. Music that is ..." She couldn't think of an appropriate word.

"Truly good," I supplied.

"Yeah, like that." She looked up at me.

I began to shake my head.

"Not a very good word?"

"No, it's not," I said. "In fact, it sucks."

Jenn started laughing. "Pam, you must think I'm a real doofus sometimes."

I think my mouth actually dropped open at that one. "Doofus?"

She laughed harder. "I just threw that one in. I knew you'd like it."

Tony Lasserman and John Robbel are already at Joanne's when I get there fifteen minutes later. Joanne is wearing an entirely different outfit than what she had decided on the phone at 7:00. A lime-green blouse and a pale yellow skirt. She looks good. If not a little scary. The black stuff around her eyes gives her this sort of bulbous-eyed, cadaverous appearance. I still haven't convinced her it isn't necessary to "bring out her eyes" that much. Tony has made a bit of an effort. His shirt is new. And his hair, normally thick and curly, lies flat against his head. Held there by about 95 tubes of gel. John, my so-called date, hasn't strained himself for the occasion. He's got a lot of mileage out of his black Nike T-shirt. I'm sure he expects to get about a million more.

We don't have to walk far. Mike lives on the street where the houses back onto the canyon. Tony and John walk behind Joanne and I. Tony wants to take a detour and see if Mrs. Marshall is still down there searching.

"I heard she isn't," says John. "I heard Mr. Marshall had her taken away to the hospital."

"Oh, yeah?"

"Yeah. She broke her foot and wouldn't go to the doctor. They took her out screaming and swearing. Mike was down there and saw the whole thing. They had to wrap her up so she wouldn't scratch anyone's eyes out. And her kids were crying. I guess it was a pretty nasty sight."

I can't help but feel sorry for Mrs. Marshall. I know she's gone quite crazy. But at least searching for Krissy gave her a shred of hope. Now she'll wake up to stare at white walls every morning.

"Ah, the kid's not down there anyway," John says with confidence. "Darla Miller's father saw her in the parking lot at the Center with a guy in a white van. By the time he called the police, the van was gone."

Joanne had heard differently. "I don't know about that. Our neighbor was walking her dog the day she disappeared. She said she saw a red Toyota leave the Canyon with a little girl wearing a pink sweater in the front passenger seat. She didn't get a good look at the driver."

Tony listens to both stories. He stuffs his hands in his pockets and shrugs. "Who knows what happened. Maybe no one ever will."

We have arrived at Ortega's. As the hand-painted sign instructs, we walk straight into the basement family room through the open garage door. Most of our class is already there. Mrs. Ortega has set up a table with a giant bowl of strawberry punch in the center of it. Huge strawberries bob around. We each fill a cup. She has strung banners, "Good Luck Graduates" and "All the Best," across the walls. She's hung streamers and curly ribbons, and sprinkled shiny confetti over the tablecloth. Mrs. Ortega is obviously really into this graduation thing.

We stand around the punch table sipping our drinks.

"My, my," Joanne says, looking around us. "It's all so civilized."

I pass Joanne a bowl of potato chips. "Pringle, my dear?"

She sniffs. "Never touch them, myself. How about a cigarette?"

"You'd better not," I tell her. "If Mike's parents don't come down on you, you know I will."

"Whatever you say, Miss Collins. No need to get tough with me." Joanne sighs. "God, I'm glad to get out of the house. This may be dry, but at least I get a break from watching my mother vacuum the halls. Linda's been hiding from me at school. If I see her, I'm going to personally pierce another hole through her big flabby lips and hook them shut with a padlock. Can you believe how she went on about what I said to Bartell in front of my mother like that? What *is* a coot, anyway? My dad won't tell me. He's kind of ticked off."

"Don't know. But I'll ask Jenn. It sounds like the kind of word she'd know."

Mandeep and Danny are playing pool at the other end of the room. Danny is useless at it. He misses the cue ball four times out of five. Mandeep is like some kind of master. You'd think she'd invented the game. She's sinking them, one after another, like she's been playing all her life.

"I think you're lying to me," Danny says to her after she sinks three in a row. He wears a big grin. "No way is this the first time you've ever played."

Mandeep is giggling as she takes aim again. "It is! No kidding. The very first time in my entire life." She sinks another ball. "I don't believe this!"

They both start laughing. They look real good together.

John and Tony are throwing darts with Mike Ortega. Mike is being seriously loud and cheerful. I think he's just trying to give his party a kick-start. Tony is throwing one bull's-eye after another. John can't even come close. Pretending frustration, John insists he needs a bigger target. "Mike, go stand against the wall, will ya? And turn around. I want to see how close I can come to your butt."

Mike laughs, "Yeah, right man." He thinks for a minute. "Hey, where's Darla Miller's brother? The guy that wears that spiked collar and combats. Didn't I see him come in? Yeah, there he is. By the bar. He's nuts enough to do it. See all those holes and rings through his skin? He'd probably get off on stopping a few darts."

They all laugh.

Darla Miller's brother *is* there, leaning against the bar, with one heavy boot resting on the rung of a stool. Linda Yip is perched on top of the stool. Sort of hidden out of sight behind his combats. I recognize her by the plume of green hair rising above his shoulder. She sticks her head into the room momentarily. Like some kind of paranoid turtle. Quickly, she glances around the room. Spotting Joanne, she instantly withdraws it. But it is too late. Joanne has seen her.

"There she is!" Joanne exclaims. She starts toward her. "I've got a few things to say to that little — "

I can only guess what they are. But I know they won't be flattering. I step in front of her. "This is a party, Jo." I raise my hand. "You know, a time to be happy. And glad. Let bygones be bygones. And old differences be forgot. Besides, do you really want to start something with somebody who's got a friend that looks like that?"

We both stare at Darla Miller's brother. Illuminated by the light above the bar, the spikes on his collar gleam threateningly. Joanne reconsiders. "Well, maybe I'll just wait until she's alone."

"Good plan." I pride myself on picking intelligent friends.

The door to the patio is open. Outside sit Sarah McMurtry, Shauna Whittaker, Carol Sanchez, Darla Miller and a bunch of guys I don't know. I leave Joanne and go outside to join them. The air is fresh and sweet in the backyard, being right on the edge of the canyon. I talk for quite a while with all of them. Even Sarah McMurtry. She no longer holds a grudge over the Barbie-doll hair-cutting thing. She tells me so. And I hold no grudge against her. It hardly seems worth it. When you're saying something as big as "so long, enjoy the rest of your life" to someone, small things can be forgotten. And that really is what we are doing. It's true, some of us will be going to the same high school. But probably only a few of us will keep in touch.

The talk turns to clothes. Specifically, graduation dresses. Carol bought hers at Holt Renfrew. Her sister helped pick it out. Shauna got hers at some boutique on Robson. The owner is a friend of her mom's. And Sarah's mom is sewing hers. Turning toward the canyon, I drift away from them. Here I am, at a party, getting that sad, all alone feeling again. I go inside to try and shake it off.

Mike's dad is just coming down the stairs carrying about ten boxes of pizza. I help him organize them on the pool table, after we cover it in a plastic cloth. I arrange the paper plates and serviettes so people can help themselves, as Mr. Ortega says, efficiently. He keeps on making this deal about what a great helper I am. How he wishes Mike would be like that. That causes Mike to give me the evil eye. I just say, "Thanks." I don't tell him how deserted I am feeling inside. How when I feel like this, keeping busy is the only way I can hang on.

Joanne and I start this game, counting how many pieces of pizza everyone eats. And how fast. Carl Jenkins wins with eight ham and pepperoni in half an hour. He slurps down two cans of pop, plops in the center of the couch and produces this enormous, gross burp. There is a distinct rumble from the other end.

"Aak," Joanne grimaces. "I still can't believe I let that walrus get close to me."

I remember her necking with Carl last fall at Darla Miller's party. "See what a few beer and several Kahlua get you? Carl Jenkins with all the sound effects."

But she isn't paying attention to me. She's looking toward the open garage door. "Oh, look who's here. Right on time. Two hours later than everyone else. Danielle Higgins."

We watch Danielle sweep into the room, and stumble over a chair.

"Hmm," says Joanne. "That wasn't too graceful. You know, I don't think she can walk straight. It seems like she's already loaded up on punch. And not the strawberry kind."

Danielle picks herself up. She gives the chair a kick like it had positioned itself just to trip her. Behind her, Matt Leighton sets it straight.

Standing in the center of the room, Danielle stretches up tall. She reaches her arms high above her head to form a Y. She stays like that, waiting for our attention. We are already more or less quiet anyway. Still intrigued by her entrance into the room.

"Happy graduation, everybody," is what I think she says, before she loses her balance and Matt steers her to a chair. I hear him quietly tell her to get a grip. Why she insisted on coming like this was just not fair to Mike. He suggests that he take her home. She laughs at the suggestion. That's when I turn away. I am angry at her for humiliating Matt like this.

I continue talking to Joanne and Mandeep. I can only hear the commotion as Danielle asks for a drink. A real drink, not that prissy pink stuff with that cherry or whatever it is bobbing up and down. Making her seasick.

"Alright, alright," I hear Mike mutter. He appeases her by sneaking one of his dad's beer from the fridge. "Keep it low. Please. My mom will blow a fuse if she finds out."

Joanne is watching all this over my shoulder. "What a miserable, self-centered bit — "

"UH-HMM," I warn her. Because behind her, Mrs. Ortega is bounding cheerfully down the stairs. I step forward.

"Oh, look, Mrs. Ortega is bringing us some games to play. Jo — Mandeep — Danny — Twister, anyone?"

It is not so much a question as a strong suggestion. I don't know why, but I feel it is my duty to protect

Matt. By drawing attention — specifically, Mrs. Ortega's attention — away from Danielle. Mrs. Ortega sets her armful of boxes down. She claps her hands together and looks happily around the room. Satisfied that everyone is having a good time, she returns back upstairs.

Nobody actually plays the games. Because we decide to social dance instead. We do the fox trot to Metallica. The swing to the Red Hot Chili Peppers. And the cha-cha to Radiohead. Mike pretends to be Mr. Bartell. With Joanne's eyeliner, he draws several scraggles on his chin. We all get a turn to dance with him. But after several songs, he needs to take a break. His eyes are sore and blurry from stretching them out of his head. I do the tango with Danny. I waltz with Tony. And I do the polka with John. To Beck. That last one is a real challenge. Now I need to cool off. I grab a Coke and head for the patio, where most of those who aren't dancing have now gravitated. I sit down with Linda and Joanne. In the last half-hour, they have become friends again.

"Is she still in there?" Joanne asks me.

"Who?"

"Danielle, the major witch. We're planning her end."

"Oh yeah? What are you going to do? Melt her?"

Linda laughs. "If it were only that easy. No, but something like that. It's got to be really big. We were thinking of a psychological approach. We'll all sit around her in a big ring. We'll blindfold her, then one by one we'll each recall aloud how she humiliated us."

"That won't work," I offer. "Do *you* really want to live through the humiliation again? Because that's what will happen. It won't bother her. She'll get off on it. She'll probably just sit there with a big smirk."

They think about this.

"Hmph," says Joanne. "Yeah. You're probably right. Well ..." She purses her lips. Wrinkles appear on her forehead. "Okay, what about this? We're changing out of our gym strip. Linda, you move into the hall. Pam, you stand in the doorway. When Danielle is all naked, I'll give the signal to you, Pam, you pass it to Linda, and Linda, you pull the fire alarm. In the confusion, I'll steal Danielle's clothes. She'll have to run out of the school naked or in a towel or whatever."

Hmm. Linda and I are not impressed.

"Naw, that's weak," I say.

Linda agrees. "Too many things could go wrong. Besides, Danielle would love it. It would give her another chance to flaunt what she's got."

"Hey, Pam." A voice interrupts our conspiring circle.

I look up to see where it is coming from. Matt Leighton is standing, tall and slightly stooped, smack in front of me.

Well, by now, you know me. And you can probably guess my initial reaction is to continue sitting there — just gawking at the delicious guy. Real stupidly. Which I do. As do both Joanne and Linda. I quickly perceive this from the absolute silence next to me. But to my credit, I am also able to revive myself before they do. When this happens, I am able to mumble, "Hi, Matt." Although my own voice sounds mega-miles away from me. I then add something else. I say, "Why don't you sit down with me?"

Bold of me, you might think. But there is something, like, no kidding, I'll use the word vulnerable, in his appearance. Maybe it's just the way his hands are stuffed all the way into his pockets. Like he doesn't know what to do with them. Or maybe it's the way this one piece of hair hangs kind of, like, waifishly over one eye. Whatever, I feel this obligation to make him feel comfortable.

"Thanks," he says. And he sits on a patio chair across from me. "So, how's Emily?" He pulls his chair toward me. He looks to his left, then leans forward with his fingers interlocked, balancing his elbows on his knees. This is to create some intimacy. Between himself and me. Mostly because Joanne and Linda continue to stare at us with their big eyes blinking and their mouths hanging wide open. Like two monster caverns, each large enough to house a colony of bats. Reluctantly, they take the hint and pretend to have something to say to each other.

"She's good," I answer to his question about Emily. "She's getting longer. Maybe one day she'll even grow into her ears."

Matt listens, but he seems distracted by something. He keeps looking over my shoulder in the direction of the patio doors. "That's nice." He starts fidgeting with his fingers. Locking them. And unlocking them.

"How's Swat?"

There is a bit of a delay before he answers. Like my question has to wrestle with whatever else is occupying his head. "Oh, good. He's good." More fidgeting. This time he focuses on his watch.

I have to ask the obvious. "Are you okay?"

"Huh? Yeah, yeah." More fidgeting. More silence.

"It's supposed to snow six inches tomorrow."

Another delay. "Really? That'll be good." His forehead crinkles ever so slightly. "What are you talking about? It's the second week of June."

I laugh. "Just testing if you're really here."

For the first time since he sat down, Matt shows his wonderful grin. "Sorry. I guess I'm not thinking very clearly."

Inside the house, I hear the music stop. More people file outside, laughing, fanning themselves with their hands, coming out to cool off.

I lean a little closer to Matt. "Is something bothering you?"

He stops fidgeting. He looks up, sort of intently at me. Like he's trying to decide if I will understand. I guess he decides that I will.

"Yeah. It's Danielle. She's not ..." He glances to his

side again, at Joanne, who is talking to someone else. "Well, let's just say it's not working out. And I don't know how to call it off. She's a very ..." he fumbles for the right word, "determined person. I don't want a big fight."

Yes! I have to try real hard to keep a helpful, concerned look when I'm, like, flying inside! He's almost free! And he's talking to me. Right here. Right now. Sharing his thoughts.

"Well," I say, and I bite my lips hard so they don't sneak into a smile and give me away. "Why not just stop calling her? After a while, she's likely to get the hint."

"That would be alright. If it wasn't her that's always calling me."

We both sit thinking about this. Which strikes me as pretty funny, considering I'd been contemplating something very similar with Joanne and Linda not too long before. Around us, the party is moving onto the patio. It's too warm in the house. Some people are wandering down toward the canyon. Concentrating on Matt's dilemma, we don't really notice the shifting people around us. We don't notice Danielle come up behind Matt. Until she slaps her arms around his shoulders.

"There you are! I've been missing you." She is really toasted now. Her hair is a mess and her eyes don't focus on anything. The lipstick she has recently stuck on gives her this crazed sort of look. "Let's get out of here." She slobbers all over him. "We'll go hide in your basement. Nobody ever goes down there." Danielle sloppily kisses him on the mouth.

I have to turn away. I can't watch anybody be that disgusting. Besides, I know that's what Matt would want me to do. He stands up suddenly, the movement throwing her off his shoulders. Danielle staggers back. Quickly recovering, she comes back with even more force.

"I know that was an accident," she says angrily. She pushes her body against his again. Matt takes her by the arms. Determinedly, he lifts her off.

"It was no accident, Danielle."

Even in her wasted state, she understands what he is saying to her. He is telling her something nobody has had the guts to tell her before. He's tired of her vanity. Hot flares jump from her hazy eyes. She is, all of a sudden, absolutely focused. Right in his face.

"You jerk! You lousy creep! How dare you push me away!" Danielle gives Matt a shove. "You disgusting animal!"

There is absolute silence. Like — noo-body moves. Nobody knows what to say.

Matt nervously rubs his forehead. "Please, Danielle," he pleads quietly. "Just let me take you home." He reaches out to touch her shoulder.

She slaps his hand away, hard. "Don't touch me! And just who are you playing around with behind my back?" Danielle turns her spiteful gaze to me. "Her?"

Like she can't believe it. "That nobody?"

Okay, this is getting way too nasty. I rise from my chair. Joanne jumps to her feet beside me.

Danielle's eyes narrow as she talks to Matt, but she doesn't lift her eyes from me. Her voice is cutting. And much steadier than her body. "Do you know something about her? She's a nutcase. She comes from a family of them. Her mother was as demented as they come."

"That's enough, Danielle." Matt's tone is flat and demanding.

"No." She ignores him. She moves a little farther away from him. And a little closer to me. "I don't think you know this about her. And you should if you're going to mess around with her. Her mother was a kook. Crazy. Psychotic. A serious wacko! Last year — huh, this will make you laugh — she took a swan dive off the suspension bridge!"

"Danielle!" Matt orders. Still, I see him look at me. He didn't know. He had absolutely no idea.

"Do you really want to get involved with someone as mentally crippled as that?!"

Joanne lunges forward, about to tear her evil heart out. I catch her by the arm and pull her back. I hold her there while she spits and swears. My eyes are stinging. My head is spinning. I feel suffocated by this major lump swelling in my throat. I fight hard — harder than I've fought for anything in my life — to hold the tears back. Several people around me are really angry. Joanne.

Linda. Sarah. John. These people, my friends. Matt tells Danielle it's time she learned to keep her great fat mouth shut. Mike tells her to get the hell out of his house. The rest just don't know what to say.

I stand there numb for what seems an eternity. Hearing the anger grow around me. It is because of me it started. It is up to me to put an end to it. Danielle's words have torn a soft wound wide open. But I'm not going to bleed all over everybody. Not on Danielle's account. Not for her entertainment. I step forward.

"Danielle." My voice sounds distant, and, thankfully, detached. Everyone stops and listens. I have to say something worth saying. Something profound. Something deadly. Something killing. "You ..." Something that proves I win. "You are ..." I hesitate only a moment. "You are ... a doofus."

Yes, I pick Jenn's word. The thing is, I don't swear. Years ago my mom told me it's not necessary to be vulgar to get your point across. You are more persuasive if you're not rude in someone's face. So, I don't. But still, I needed something really obnoxious. And doofus was the last obnoxious word I had in my head. Thanks to Jenn.

At first there is astonished silence around me. Then a few snickers. Then uproarious laughter — from everyone. All at Danielle's expense. She glows red in the darkness. Sways a bit, and drops lifelessly into a chair. The laughter continues.

But I don't laugh with them. The wound inside aches painfully. I can't continue to keep the tears from spilling out. I know I'm very close to falling apart. Before it happens, I want to be far, far away from here. I head for the door. But before I get to it, there is a shout from down by the canyon. We hear it again, this time several steps closer.

"Hey!" It is Danny Kim. "Hey!" He and Mandeep stumble breathlessly onto the patio. Danny is carrying something. "Look what I found!" And he holds up a small pink sweater.

That's all it takes. At the sight of that small pink sweater, the tears I'd been stifling come rushing out. I duck through the door. I run out through the basement, through the garage and I don't stop until I'm in my own house.

Dad and Jenn are watching a movie in the living room. I charge past them, straight to my bedroom, where I crumble onto my bed. How could anyone in this world be so mean and horrible? Within minutes I am nothing but a damp, sobbing mess. Dad and Jenn appear in the doorway.

"Pam? Why are you home so early? Pam? Pammy? Oh, sweetheart, what's wrong?" Dad sits down on the bed and pulls me close to him. Jenn leaves the room and quietly closes the door. "What's wrong, honey?"

Although I can hardly talk and I probably don't make much sense, I tell Dad everything that happened at the party.

"Oh, Pam." He tries to brush my tears away. "She's just a very mean, selfish person. You can't let those kind of people get to you. I know it's hard. But you're better off to try and ignore what she said."

"I don't care about her, Dad." I sniffle and snurf. I am really having a problem trying to get myself together. "I want to know why she did it."

Dad appears sort of puzzled. "Well, you just told me. Because you were talking to her boyfriend. She didn't like that."

"I don't mean her!" I take a deep breath before falling apart again. "I mean Mom. Why did she do it? Why did she do this to me?"

I feel Dad draw me closer. He strokes my hair and rocks me just a little. He doesn't say anything. I don't think he can. It's a question to which even he doesn't have an answer.

"I mean, why didn't she want to be with me? She'd only known April for eight months. She couldn't even walk yet. She'd known me my entire life. Didn't she love me anymore? Why did she want to be with April and not me?"

"Is that what you think?" Dad holds me away from him so he can look at my face. I see the tears fill his own sad eyes. I feel guilty. He'd been happily watching a movie with Jenn. And here I am dragging him down with me.

Dad takes a shaky breath. "Oh, Pam." He hugs me again. "It was exactly because she loved you so much that, in her depressed mind, she felt you'd be better off without her. That I'd be better off without her. It was a terrible symptom of her illness. Do you remember your last walks in the canyon together?"

How could I ever forget them in my entire life? I can only nod.

"She'd come home and hurt so badly. She'd cry on those nights. You know why? Because you were so enthusiastic. You tried so hard to get her to enjoy those walks the way she used to. And she just couldn't. She felt she let you down. She didn't think she could ever make you happy again."

We are both crying now.

"Well, now for sure she can't."

Dad shakes his head. "No. I know you think that now. But let me tell you something, dear. Your mother was a beautiful, intelligent, caring woman, who, before she became ill, laughed easily. She loved life. Perhaps more than anyone I've ever known. You are absolutely like her. You have her sense of humor. You have her love of life. She will always be a part of you. It's because of her that one day you will laugh at life again."

"Think so?" I've cried so hard my whole insides ache.

"I know so."

After a while, Dad moves to my desk chair. We talk about Mom until long after midnight. Dad tells me a lot of things about her that I never knew before. Things about her when she was a teenager. A little bit older than me right now. How she won a ribbon at the school science fair for her display of the leaves of British Columbia's rainforests. How when they were in university, they'd go for walks in Lynn Canyon. Mom would break off root licorice from the moss that grows on the vine maples and peel it for Dad to try. This makes me start to cry all over again. After I thought the tears were all used up. I've cried a lot tonight. And Dad has cried a lot. But somehow, I feel so much better. And I think he does too.

"Tell me again what you called her?" Dad asks, long after our tears are exhausted.

I kind of smile. "A doofus."

Dad can't stop laughing. "I would have loved to see the look on her face."

NINETEEN

June 14th

Last night I dreamed that I was walking with Mom in Lynn Canyon Park. It was sunny and warm and we were walking with our arms around each other, just meandering down the path. We were chewing root licorice and looking for the woodpecker Mom heard high up in a cottonwood. We weren't in any particular hurry to get anywhere. And as we walked, we talked about everything that's happening in my life right now. Just so unbelievably matter-of-fact. We talked about what my friends are up to, and how I'm doing at school, and what my teachers are like. Funny thing is, she knew all about what was going on with me. She knew I had to dance with Mr. Bartell. She knew about the man who chased me. She knew Danny was going through a rough time. She knew Joanne was grounded. She knew how I had stood up to Danielle. She knew all that. And in my dream, it didn't surprise me that she knew, it seemed only normal that she would.

We talked about my new puppy, Emily. She was all excited about that. I told her about Jennifer Reid and how Dad seemed quite happy these days. She smiled and said she was glad. She told me Dad is a very good man. He deserves someone like Jennifer who can make him feel like that.

She hoped that Nana Jean was well and that I made a point of calling her now and again. I said that I would. We continued walking, until we came to a branch in the path. I knew she had to go a different way than me. I knew I had to continue on toward the wooden bridge all alone.

We stopped. She took her arm from around me, but still she held my hand. Somehow, in my dream, I knew I had to speak fast. I told her how much I missed her. I told her how much I loved her. I told her how I couldn't believe she was gone. Just gone from my life like that. I told her how much I wished that she would come back.

She smiled again and stroked my cheek. "I love you too." And then, she let go of my hand. She began to move away from me. "But you're doing just fine, my little girl. Just fine ... just fine ... my little Pam ... "

"Mom!" I was awake in my bed.

TWENTY

August 15ᵗʰ

Danny Kim is sort of a hero. It was because he discovered Krissy's sweater that her body was found late that night. She had made it all the way to the end of the canyon. To where the houses back onto it. But there is a cliff she had to climb in order to get out. She tried. But, perhaps too weak, she stumbled. Her sweater snagged on the blackberry bush where Danny found it. She fell back to the canyon floor, hitting her little head on a rock on the way down.

It seemed like half the city turned out for her funeral. I saw it on the news. Her family and classmates and teachers. The many, many people who searched for her. And many who didn't know her at all. There were piles and piles of beautiful flowers. Mrs. Marshall was brought to the funeral in a wheelchair. The rest of the family looked like they could hardly stand up. I fell to pieces watching them. It was impossible not to.

I have tried to imagine what Krissy's final few hours were like. All alone. Just her tiny self against this canyon. What a tough little girl she must have been. Being lost and cold and hungry is one thing. But this place — it is a terrifying place if you let it overwhelm you. It is wild and wicked, with things snarling in the shadows. Things creeping from the mossy forest floor. The sound of water crashing against granite. From hundreds of feet above. And Lynn Creek always roaring. All day. All night. All year. Always. We are nothing compared to these two giants of nature — the water and the rock. Yet despite this, Krissy almost made it out. She is another victim of Lynn Canyon. Her family are victims of Lynn Canyon. Like Mom. Like me. Like Dad. Victims, and maybe, in a way, heros, of this terrible, beautiful place.

I'm trying to get Emily to sit on the rock beside me. Down here at Ninety Foot. But it's not going to happen, I can see. She keeps pulling at the leash, digging at this root, yanking me down this path, sniffing at the slugs. This is Emily's favorite place in the whole world. She nags me to come down here every day. I knew she was smart the moment I saw her. You should see how she drags her leash from the peg where it hangs in the hall when she wants to come down here for a walk. Matt usually comes with us in the afternoons. Quite often, he brings Swat. But he's working today and Joanne's gone shopping with her mom. So I'm all alone. That's alright. I don't mind just this once.

I've been seeing Matt since the night of Mike Ortega's party. He apologized for days after the party for what Danielle said to me. He's still apologizing.

"Matt. Quit it," I told him a week ago. "You are hardly responsible for what came out of her mouth."

"I should never have let her talk me into going that night. What she said was horrible. She was horrible."

"Yes, you're right, she was. But, you know, looking back on it, maybe it wasn't all bad."

"What do you mean?"

"I mean, it made me begin to fight back."

Matt looked puzzled.

I glinted at him. "Swat wants you to throw the stick again."

Joanne and the rest of my friends were real proud of me. They said it was just the best comeback they'd ever heard.

"It was just so ... so ... goofy, it cracked us up! I mean, like, in light of the tenseness of the situation and everything. It was perfect. Doofus!" Joanne wiped a tear from her eye, leaving a long black smudge across her face. "Pam, nobody but you could have stayed so cool."

Yeah, right. I was totally cool. At ease. If they only knew.

I'm just glad this year is over. I feel somehow that I'm awakening from it. That I'm standing up and shaking myself off. Opening up a bit. Beginning to move on. But then, maybe like the seeds popping open and the leaves unfurling, it's been happening all along.

Our graduation banquet was held at the Hotel Vancouver. Matt and me and Dad and Jenn all went together. We sat at a table with Joanne and Tony and both of their parents. Dad gets along real well with Matt. They started talking about sports cars, which it turns out Matt knows a lot about, and nobody could get a word in all night.

Oh, and Dad and Jenn gave me the coolest grad presents. They bought me my own copy of Emily Carr's journals. And get this — a print of "Mountain Forest." Jenn had it framed and everything. It's beautiful. I hung it on the wall so I can look at it when I'm lying on my bed.

"How did you know?" I asked her.

"You spent a long time looking at it in the Art Gallery. It must mean something to you."

"Yes," I nodded. "It does."

Matt also brought me a present. When I opened the door the night of the banquet, he was standing there with, like, this real coy look on his face. He shifted his feet and moved his hands, which were hiding behind his back.

"I have something for you. It's not much. But I was thinking of you."

"Thank you."

He continued to stand there.

"Well, what is it?"

He brought his hands out from behind his back. With a grin, he held up a baby-food jar. It was full of water. "Ninety Foot. You don't have one."

I took the jar from him. Holding it in my hands, feeling its coolness, I almost started to cry.

My sniveling made him nervous.

"Well, like I said, it's not much. I just thought if you ever move away from here ... you know, you'd want it."

I nodded. "Thanks, Matt. I do want it. I want it very much."

Jenn says I have every right to be angry. She says I've suffered more death in my fourteen years than anybody should. She says very few people have to deal with what I'm dealing with, and if people stumble around me, it's only because they don't know.

"Golly, Pam. Nobody can see the part of you that's been ripped wide open. Nobody can know how much it aches. You have every reason in this world to feel hurt and abandoned. You have every right to cry whenever you want."

Golly, Jenn. Thanks. What you said just now really kind of helps. Now I don't feel like I'm so weird. Like, when I do have a moment, I'm not just some kind of wimp that can't cope. And I still have them. I have them a lot. I suppose I'll keep on having them, for who knows, maybe even the rest of my life. I can't imagine this kind of hurt ever completely healing. Not without some kind of scar. You know something else, Jenn? You're okay. In fact, I like you quite a lot.

It was good I had that talk with Dad after the party. It was the first time we'd really opened up. We had been so concerned about upsetting one another that we had avoided talking about Mom. Each of us afraid that even mentioning her might cause the other to really crack. What frightened us most, we agreed, was shattering the fragile order of our existence. The order we had created to make it from one day to the next.

I'm glad he told me about how Mom is really a part of me. I don't come down here to Lynn Canyon to visit her anymore. Now, I bring her with me. I will always try to remember she's a part of me. When I'm missing her. When my friends go shopping with their moms. When they're standing next to them, hugging them, crying at their graduations or their weddings. I'll try real hard to remember that my mom is inside me. I won't need her there in body. I'll just know what she would have thought or felt or said. Rats. This is going to be so hard.

Mom taught me so much in our time together. But there's one thing she taught me that she didn't even know. From her death I have learned it. I have learned that no matter how bad, how really rotten your life gets — I mean, like, it just couldn't get any worse — there is always hope. Things will always get better. I know that now. I know that they will. They are. I only wish someone had taught *you* that, Mom.

I have been thinking about my future. I've pretty much ruled out becoming a shiftless drifter. I'm keeping my options open. I'm taking both arts and sciences in high school. Mr. Bartell helped me decide on that. "Never limit yourself, Pamela. Keep all your doors open. You just never know what life's going to throw at you. Take me, for instance. I'm one fabulous English teacher. But if English teachers go the way of the dinosaur, man, can I ballroom dance!"

Right. Whatever you say, Mr. Bartell.

Whatever I do with my life, I'm going to be good at it. I've made that much of a decision. I'm going to live life and love life. Like you did, Mom. I'm going to stand up on this white rock and yell orders to the canyon. I don't care if it can't hear me. I'm going to plunge deep into the frigid waters of Ninety Foot. I'm going to climb these purple mountains. I'm going to breathe in, suck in, all this heaving earth around me. I'm going to grab onto a wing and fly high up there — way up there — with the peregrine falcons. With you, Mom. No kidding. You and me are going to do it. You and me. We will.